HONORING HIS LADY (A MEDIEVAL ROMANCE)

NORFOLK KNIGHTS—BOOK 5

SASKIA KNIGHT

—Norfolk Knights—

Claiming his Lady (Novella)
Seducing his Lady (Novella)
Awakening his Lady (Novella)
Defending his Lady (Full-length novel)
Honoring his Lady (Full-length novel)

You can sign up to Saskia's newsletter via her website for more information on book releases.

For more information about this author visit:
www.saskiaknight.com

NOTES ON NORFOLK

Today, Norfolk is a quiet, rural county in eastern England, criss-crossed with narrow roads, golden fields, and full of tantalizing reminders of a very different past. With over 659 medieval churches still standing, you can't help but reflect on a time when Norfolk was rich, heavily populated and a very different place to the one in which I grew up!

To help you figure out where the books in the Norfolk Knights series are set, I've created the map below. The first three books featuring Rowena, Melisende, and Angelique are set in and around the medieval ports of Blakeney Haven and Cley, close to where I was raised. Book 4 onwards are set on the coast, near the rivers and Broads of east Norfolk.

Wherever I live, Norfolk will always be my home and I'm happy that I can share a little of my love for it with you through the stories of the three Gresham sisters, and the de Vere family.

Happy reading!

Saskia

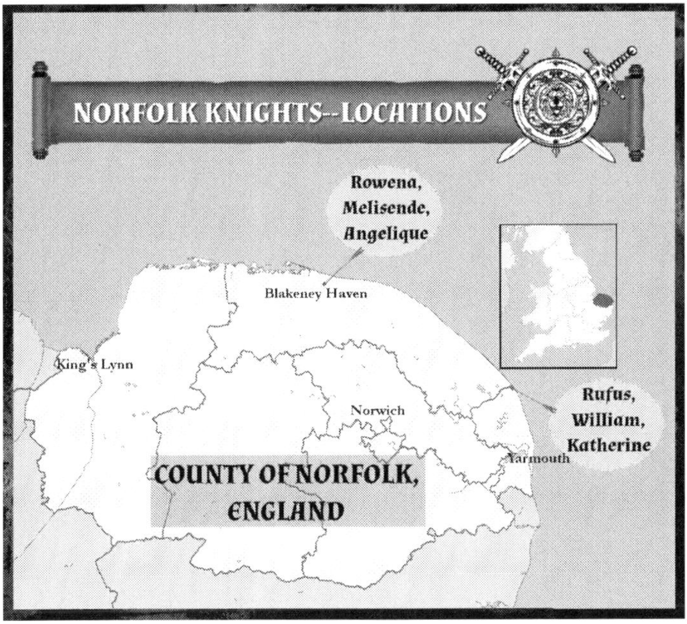
NORFOLK KNIGHTS--LOCATIONS
Rowena,
Melisende,
Angelique
Blakeney Haven
King's Lynn
Norwich
Rufus,
William,
Katherine
Yarmouth
COUNTY OF NORFOLK,
ENGLAND

PROLOGUE

Norfolk, 1198

Thirteen-year-old Lady Alice de Courcy ran through the field of swaying crops beside her castle home without a backward glance. Her unbound, fair tresses flew behind her, rivaling the golden barley in their brightness.

Despite the fierce summer sun, she continued to run until she reached the woods. There the sunlight became dappled and the air fresher as she arrived at the stream where she always met her best friend, William. He was there, waiting for her as usual.

"Alice," he greeted, with his customary brevity, and shy smile. She often wondered how he managed to convey so much in so few words. She'd decided it was because his eyes were so expressive—a deep brown, as brown as the soil in winter, fringed with thick dark lashes. They were eyes you could trust.

"William," she said, placing her hand against her chest as she tried to regain her breath. "Goodness! It was not easy to get away today. The castle is in an uproar, and Mother is even more bad-tempered than usual."

She waited for him to ask why, but he simply continued to lean against one of the gnarly old oaks, and watch her, a slight smile playing on his lips.

"Are you not interested to know why?" she asked.

"Aye, if you wish to tell me."

She shrugged. "Nay, if you don't wish to know, then I shall not tell you, even if it is most interesting," she teased.

She took a few steps away as if she might wander along the stream, before dropping to her knees to admire a clump of bright wildflowers. She stroked the buttery yellow petals, aware of William behind her. He knelt beside her, plucked a flower, and offered it to her.

"What should I do with it?" she asked, wanting to provoke him into something more than distant admiration.

"Place it behind your ear. It will look pretty."

"*You* should place it there." She didn't know who was more shocked, her for uttering such flirtatious words, or the very proper William. He'd never touched her other than to hold her hand when they were younger. For the last few years, though, even that had stopped, much to her frustration.

Their gazes locked as he did as she bid, and brushed her hair aside with his long, calloused fingers, and gently slid the flower behind her ear. She watched his throat convulse as he swallowed. He stepped away and sat against a tree, his eyes still on her.

"So?" she asked.

"So?" he repeated.

"Does it look pretty?"

"Alice," he said, with a warning narrowing of the eyes. "You know it does."

"I know nothing of the sort."

"Well, now you do."

"I suppose I do. So"—she spread her skirts prettily around her—"now we're here, what shall we do?" She knew what she wanted him to do. She wanted him to kiss her like she'd seen the stable boy kiss her maid.

"Talk?" he suggested.

She sighed. "I suppose so. Of what shall we talk?"

"You can tell me what you wanted to tell me earlier."

"Oh, that. It is nothing. Simply my father's cousin is coming to stay while my father is in London."

William frowned. "Why is your father in London?"

Alice shrugged. "He says he's needed there. But I heard my mother tell her sister that it was good riddance."

"But what about the land?"

Alice laughed. "That is so like you, William. Your first thought is always for the land."

William smiled, too. He wasn't like the other youths who hated to be laughed at. She'd told him that once, and he'd replied that indeed he was, but somehow she could say anything, and he didn't mind.

"As it should be, Alice. For it is the land which gives us life." He raked his fingers through the rich earth and rubbed it between his fingers, letting it shower to the ground.

For some reason, she was stirred by the way he fingered the soil so tenderly.

"Anyone would think you love the soil more than people. More than *a* person," she couldn't help adding.

He raised those dark eyes to her, and her heart stopped.

"More than most, that much is true, but not more than you."

She turned away to hide her smile. It made her feel good when he said things like that. She'd always known he'd liked her best of all girls. It would have been hard not to know, for he'd been telling her thus ever since she was a child. But in recent years, although he'd never tried to kiss or caress her, his admissions of love made her feel something else, something quite different.

She lay on the soft grass and closed her eyes, aware that his eyes were upon her. "Listen to the birds singing! Isn't it glorious? Like the choir in Norwich Cathedral."

The grasses rustled as William lay beside her. She stretched her fingers out and held her breath, wondering if he would do as she wished. When she felt the tentative touch of his fingers upon her own, she released a long sigh and opened her eyes. He curled his fingers around hers and swept his thumb along the side of her hand, circling twice around the nail of her little finger. She'd never known a sensation like it. It was as if he touched other parts of her. For one long moment, neither moved.

Later, when she remembered that moment, she could have sworn that the birds had stopped singing, that the leaves, high above them in the tree's canopy, had stopped moving, that the air had been sucked from her body. And later still she'd wished with all her heart that her life had ended then, with such sweetness.

But, instead, a darkness came upon them. A cloud slid across the sun at the same time as they became aware of the sound of a horse's hooves drumming into the ground upon which they lay. It was William who jumped up first, looking toward the woodland path along which a horseman was riding.

Alice stood behind William as the stranger approached, spotted them, and pulled his great destrier to a savage halt. Alice shivered as the stranger's eyes swept over her.

"You must be Alice." His voice was no friendlier than his eyes.

She swallowed. "Indeed, sir."

"I offered to find you when your mother said you were missing."

The chill Alice felt didn't leave her, but she curtseyed as she'd been taught. She had no idea who this man was but could tell he was accustomed to being obeyed. He had not the appearance of a lackey.

"Come," he said, "we can ride together back to the castle."

"Thank you, sir, but I can walk."

He leaned down, and she didn't like the way his breath smelled of brandy. His hand came around hers and grasped it tight. "Back to the castle with you, little maid." He pulled her up in front of him, and she clung to the horse's mane.

She turned to William, who glowered at the man, his fists clenched. It wasn't like him. Her world had turned upside down.

"Alice, I—" shouted William.

But whatever William said was cut off as the stranger grasped her around the waist with one hand, and shouted at his horse to canter away.

WILLIAM WATCHED the only girl he'd ever loved taken away from him by a stranger. He was panting with anger. Sweat beaded his face, and yet he felt a sickening chill settle deep inside. Something was wrong, and he knew not what it was. But the same feeling he had about the soil which he loved so much, told him the truth about Alice.

There were three things he knew without words: one the land, and two, his beloved Alice. Something threatened Alice, but he, as a mere sixteen-year-old youngest son with no prospects, was powerless to either identify it or remedy it. But he'd do as he always did, he'd watch out for her.

One day she would be his. That was the third thing he knew.

CHAPTER 1

Autumn, 1205, Norfolk

William cantered into the bailey yard at Wanham Castle and jumped off his horse. God's bones, he was hot. He squinted up at the blue sky where high clouds were beginning to form and was thankful his day's work was done. It would rain later. He felt it. He'd been out on the land since sun up, making sure that the last of the harvest had been brought in before the heavens opened.

He tossed the reins to the stable boy and walked across to the pump, pulling off his shirt as he went. One of the maids quickly detoured from the pigsty where she had left some kitchen scraps, dropped the basket, and primed the pump for him.

They exchanged a smile, while the stable lad glowered behind them, as he obediently took William's horse to water. William shook his head.

"You should marry him and put him out of his misery, Mary."

She glanced casually at the back of the lad in question. "Simon? He's but a lad." She took William's shirt from him. The water began to flow into a bucket, and William took both handles and waited for it to fill.

"And you're naught but a lass, so you'll be well suited."

"I'd be better suited to someone taller and stronger, methinks," she said, blatantly eyeing his chest. It swelled as he took a deep breath, readying himself for the shock of cold water against his heated skin. It wasn't the only thing to swell. Mary's gaze could raise the dead, and he certainly wasn't that. Her gaze slipped lower, and her mouth tweaked with merriment. She raised lusty eyes to his. "Anytime you'd like a roll in the hay, Sir William, let me know." He shook his head and flung the bucket of cold water over his head. He gasped as it poured over his hot, sweaty body. And so did Mary, whose ripe bosoms swelled with a big sigh as her eyes swept him from head to toe once more.

He'd lain with wenches but had always made sure that they weren't Wanham wenches. He was destined for another, and one, he was sure, who wouldn't take kindly to hear of his exploits in bed. Or in the field, come to that.

He tossed his head back, sending droplets of water flying into the sultry air. He thrust his fingers through his hair and slicked it off his face. "I thank you for your offer, Mary. But I have eyes for another."

She shrugged. "Don't you fret. Lady Alice need know nothing about it. Besides, she's a lady, and what do ladies know of tumbling?"

William didn't know the answer to that. His sister-in-law, Kezia, had seemed to take to tumbling very well with his brother, Rufus. And, although she hadn't been raised a lady, it turned out she'd been born one. He hoped that his Alice might show the same interest in coupling as Kezia.

William jerked his head to the stable. "Wed Simon, that is my advice to you, Mary."

He plucked his shirt from her hands and dried off the excess moisture before running up the steps to the castle's Hall, leaving Mary scowling behind him. He pushed open the heavy oak door and breathed in the smell of beeswax and fresh herbs. His sister, Katherine, now the lady of the castle, made sure to continue to adhere to their mother's high standards. The morning sun streamed through the open shutters, revealing the luster of the well-oiled table upon which Katherine worked.

"You're back early and washed already!" exclaimed his sister, Lora, looking him up and down. "It's not yet past the middle of the day! What ails you, Will?"

"You'd have me work all the hours God sends?"

Lora shrugged. "You always do. What's so different about today?"

He didn't want to answer and so, instead, feigned interest in Katherine's accounts. She looked up and absently rubbed the ink from her fingers. William noticed shadows beneath her eyes. The eldest of his sisters had borne the brunt of the work since his mother's death. "Is the last of the harvest brought in?" she asked.

"Aye," he said. "And it's been a good one, despite the men we diverted to fight for the de Courcy castle." He accepted a glass of ale.

"It was necessary and successful," said Lora. "Alice and her mother are back living in their home. Shame her father didn't live to see it."

"Aye. That last battle proved too much for him."

"But I hear Sir Bayard of Wrotham is living at the castle again. Apparently, Lady de Courcy invited him." Lora sniffed. "That man is as slippery as an eel. One minute he's fighting against the de Courcys—and us—the next he's ingratiated himself back into their home."

"Aye, well, hopefully not for long," said William. He'd never liked Sir Bayard, but now, at least, his dislike had been vindicated. The man was a turncoat traitor.

"Why?" asked Celestria, his youngest sister. "Do you know something we don't? Because I heard he was helping Lady de Courcy find a match for Alice."

William looked up sharply. "And why would he do that?"

Celestria shrugged. "I know not. I'm merely repeating what I've heard."

"Well, don't," said Katherine, with uncharacteristic ill humor. "You're obsessed with marriage."

"It's natural," replied Celestria, unperturbed by the scolding. "You should be too."

"What is it, Katherine?" asked William. "Nothing wrong with our trade, is there?"

Katherine rubbed her neck. "It could be better. It's not as good as when Mother was alive. Her name made things happen. But some have stuck by us."

"And why would they not?" William asked. "Our word is good. You worry too much, Kat. You'll see. All will be well."

Katherine twisted her full lips into a rueful smile. "And you always see things too simply, Will."

He put his hand on her, willing his strength to travel to her slender shoulders, which always took on more of a burden than they should. "That's because they *are* simple."

Celestria, who had been playing with one of the dogs, looked up sharply. "Then why is it *you* are not married yet?"

William ignored the barb. Unlike his brothers and Lora, he and Katherine didn't rise to Celestria's sharp tongue and quick wit. He exchanged a glance with Katherine, but for once, his reliable sister didn't brush off Celestria's comment.

Katherine pushed the papers away, stood up and

smoothed down her skirts. "Celestria has a point, Will. There's nothing to stand between you and Alice now."

William held out his cup, and a maid replenished his ale. It gave him time to think because, for once in his life, he'd determined upon a course of action which he wasn't willing to share. "Now that Alice's mother no longer wishes her to marry Rufus?"

Celestria gave a sharp laugh. "That was never going to happen. Anyone who'd heard Rufus and Kezia at night would know that."

"Celestria!" reprimanded Katherine. "And how would you know of such things?"

Celestria rolled her eyes. "I have ears, sister—ears to hear Kezia's cries of passion." She dramatically hugged herself, imitating actions that William hoped she knew nothing of. "And ears to hear the servants' gossip." She stepped closer, her beautiful eyes wide. "Did you know that often, Hawise said—and she would know because she lay closest to their door—that Kezia made the sound of passion all night until dawn came."

"Celestria!" Both William and Katherine's voices combined.

Celestria flung her hands in the air. "What? It is only natural."

"It might be nature, but you are a lady and should behave like one," said Katherine.

Celestria grunted in disapproval but knew not to speak back to Katherine. For all her quietness, Katherine retained a quiet dignity that everyone respected and depended on, including William.

William watched as Celestria surveyed the Hall and wondered where her quick mind would alight next. It was soon apparent. "I don't see what you're waiting for, Will. I'd want any man of mine to come and claim me immediately he was free!"

"Alice isn't you," he said briefly, hoping that would end the conversation. He turned to Katherine. "I thought I'd check on the far fields this afternoon before the rains come."

The corners of Katherine's lips tweaked slightly, but she didn't meet his gaze. He could rely on Katherine. "I think that's an excellent idea, Will. You might want to ride over to where our lands border the Abbey's first."

Celestria called the dog over and flounced away. "That's all you two think about—land, land, land."

"It is the land that feeds you," said Katherine quietly.

"And the land which keeps me," said Celestria, disconsolately rubbing her dog's head while looking out the open door. "Without a decent dowry, Sir Geoffrey d'Anvers will never have me. And he's so handsome and so rich! Savari said all the women are wild for him at court."

Katherine didn't meet William's eye again, but he knew her thoughts on the subject of Celestria's affianced. They were the same as his. They had sufficient dowry but didn't want a man such as him in their lives. There had been some kind of tenuous arrangement between the two families when their father had been alive, but they'd let it drop. And Sir Geoffrey appeared to have no qualms doing the same. Especially as his charm had ingratiated him with the King, opening up more ambitious marriage plans, no doubt.

"We will find someone worthy of you, Celestria, never fear." Someone, he didn't say, who he hoped could cope with Celestria's barely tamed nature and sharp intellect. "I must go." He glanced up at the sky. "It is time."

Celestria's eyes narrowed slightly. William knew the warning sign. She thought she was on to something. "Time?"

Katherine cleared her throat. "Time to get back to work, as you should be doing. Have you finished your lessons?"

As Celestria prepared to demonstrate, no doubt correctly,

that she needed no further lessons from the tutor, William stepped outside, into the busy bailey yard. He surveyed the scene quickly and nodded in quick satisfaction. His father and mother might be gone, his brother settled in Sicily with his new wife, but, between him and Katherine, Wanham castle and its lands were doing well. More than well. Especially with the trade that his mother had established and which Katherine had so ably continued.

He crossed the yard, sending a chicken squawking into a pile of clean hay. Mary appeared from the stables with a self-satisfied smile, plucking some hay from her hair. She'd obviously followed his advice. William didn't regret turning down her offer. It wasn't that he was immune to the seductions of the flesh, but there had only ever been one woman for him. *One* woman. The woman he would marry. The woman he would have a yard full of squabbling children with. A woman to whom he could now lay claim.

His horse was already saddled awaiting him. For he'd made plans, plans his sisters knew naught of—although Katherine suspected and had given him advice on where he might find Alice—because he knew Celestria was right. It *was* time to claim what he wanted.

LADY ALICE DE COURCY took a calming breath as the gates to the Priory clunked shut behind her. She didn't turn around. There wouldn't have been any point anyway. The gatekeeper's disinterested gaze was always the same no matter upon whom he looked—his only interest was in discerning danger. And Lady Alice presented no threat to anyone, only herself.

She tried not to think of the haven she'd left behind. She knew from experience that dwelling on what she could not have was not the way forward. She flicked the reins of her white palfrey, who didn't appear to have the same focus as herself, distracted by the berries on the bush—lush and ripe —which had somehow escaped the nuns' attention.

She and her maid and guard rode silently alongside the Priory walls. Peeping over the top were the sun-scorched tips of the espaliered pears, their leaves withered and ready to fall as autumn advanced steadily across the land. And, like the fruit which had been harvested, Alice also felt the advent of autumn, as she faced her own fate—marriage.

She had tried everything, but her guardian was adamant —no more delays. Even the persuasion of the Abbess had come to naught. All Alice's work in creating medicines based on Islamic texts, translated by French scholars, which had helped the Priory become known for its healing, appeared to mean nothing to her guardian. He saw in her only a means of securing more wealth and prestige. The uncertain times had seen more than one suitor disappear, either falling out of favor because of the ever-changing preferences of the King, or dying, rarely from natural causes. And so her life had continued—spending her days doing worthwhile things at the Priory, and her evenings trying to bolster her mother's spirits since her father's death. She'd managed to hold out until now. And now, it seemed, her time had run out. Her guardian—her father's cousin—Sir Bayard of Wrotham, had returned and refused her plea to become a nun. Instead, he insisted she marry. While the thought terrified her, living with her Sir Bayard scared her more.

She took another calming breath, breathing in the warm autumn air, rich with crushed fruit, the buzz of bees, and the smell of dried grass. She could face whatever came to her. She was so deep in thought that to begin with she didn't hear her guard call her. It was only after a further call that she turned to him.

"My lady! A rider approaches."

Alice snapped her head around and suddenly heard the

trot of a horse's hooves upon dry packed earth. She'd been facing the wrong way, of course. Her deaf left ear was not picking up the rider's approach; her good right ear was attuned to the sounds of nature coming from the other side of the Priory walls, her senses tuned inwards, as usual.

Her guard took his place in front of her. But Alice recognized the heavy beat of the horse upon the packed earth. Her mother had often accused her of being a witch for knowing what she knew without hearing. But since she'd been struck by deafness, Alice had become more aware of things around her. Besides, she trusted the acute sensitivities of her mare, whose ears now perked up as she strained to greet the oncoming rider.

"Nay, hold back. It is William."

Outwardly, she knew there would be no sign of her response to William's approach, but inwardly her heart increased in time to the horse's canter. When he came around the corner of the Priory wall, she managed not to over-react to his warm smile.

Instead, she smiled politely, even as she took in every inch of his face, scanning it for difference, and relieved to find it the same. Mayhap a few more lines around the eyes, where his face creased into his nut-brown skin, a lighter shade of his dark brown eyes. Eyes, she'd once thought, she could sink into, but not now.

"William," she said, with a scarce nod of her head.

His smile wavered a little, but she didn't allow any warmth to leach into her chill greeting. There was no point, and there was every reason to discourage him.

"Lady Alice," he greeted, swinging down from his horse with the graceful ease of a fit man. He walked up to her and held on to the reins of her palfrey. Her horse dipped her head and whinnied in pleasure as William stroked her nose and patted her neck. Alice was pretty sure she'd have done the same. She cleared her throat, willing the errant thought to disappear from whence it had come.

"Sir William." She licked her lips as her mind raced, trying to say things other than what she felt. "You are far from your land this afternoon."

"Aye. I have other errands to do this day."

Her heart skipped a beat. "At the Priory? I believe the Abbess will be at prayers now."

"Nay. Not the Priory. I came to see you."

For a fraction of a second, they were as they'd been years before, the understanding between them complete. There were only the two of them, his kind, safe eyes searching hers, and she about to respond. In the old days, she would have. She'd have laughed out loud, able to hear everything people said to her. She'd have teased him for his unerring reliability, and they'd have talked of their future. But that was then.

She gave her head a short, sharp shake, as much to rid it of its memories, as to negate his speech. "Me?" She gave a light shrug. "How can I help? Does Katherine need medicine?"

His brows lowered, and a shadow fell across his face. His eyes, as dark and as steady as an oak tree in winter, were hidden now. "Nay. Katherine needs no medicine. We are all well. Mayhap she is more tired than usual."

"She takes on too much."

"She takes on her own duties, as well as those of lady of the manor. But she won't need to do these soon. Not when I'm married."

It was as if a dagger had pierced her, pushing its sharp blade deep inside. She only just stopped herself from pressing her hand to her gut, where the pain had come to rest.

"You mean to marry?" she asked dully.

He nodded. "I do."

She tried out a smile, but her lips failed to respond. "So, I shall be able to congratulate your new wife soon."

His brow contracted further. "Why do you speak so?"

She glanced uneasily behind her. "We must continue," she said to her guard. She looked back at William. "My mother expects me."

He released his hold, and his frown deepened. "Then I will escort you to the castle."

"There's no need."

"The mere fact that you say that shows me there's every need." He nodded to the guard and her maid. "Ride ahead and inform Lady de Courcy that I will be paying my respects shortly."

Alice bit her lip and looked from William to her maid and then back to William.

"I'm afraid that won't be possible. My mother has company this evening."

William waited, but she didn't elaborate. She didn't want William to know his identity. He grunted. "Well, another day, perhaps."

She nodded, knowing her days at the de Courcy castle were numbered.

"But mayhap, you'll at least allow me to escort you home, give leave of your companions to return ahead of us?"

She couldn't resist. A short time in which she'd have William to herself. This might be the last time. She turned to her guard and maid. "Go ahead." Alice waited until they'd cantered off before turning back to William, who'd re-mounted his horse. "And how are your sisters?"

He raised an eyebrow as they walked their horses side by side, their pace slowed as if by mutual consent. "They are well, as you know. You saw Katherine yesterday, did you not?"

"Aye." She bit back her words.

William pushed away an overhanging bough from her path. "Then," he said, squinting up into the sun, rather than look at her, "why do you ask?"

"I am…" She hesitated. "Making conversation. As people do."

"As people do," he repeated slowly, plucking a stray piece of tall grass which grew from the bank and chewing it. "And we are simply 'people' to each other?"

Alice blinked, not knowing how to answer.

Their horses moved a half-dozen steps while their riders said nothing. Her horse began to walk alongside his, seemingly responding to his magnetism as women did. But not her, never her, not now. She swallowed and drew herself a little taller in the saddle. It was William who broke the silence because Alice knew not how.

"You do not answer, Alice."

"That is because I cannot."

Casually he leaned over and took hold of her horse's reins. It stopped immediately. She had no choice but to look up into his face. "Cannot, or will not?"

She shook her head in confusion as a wave of fear filled her. Fear for what she was about to lose. His brows beetled, and then something happened for which she wasn't prepared. She saw the fear reflected in his own eyes.

"What is it, Alice? What has happened? I know we have not been close for a long while. But we had no chance. And now, with Rufus gifting the lands and title to me, surely your mother will no longer object."

She held up her hand. She had to make him stop. "Enough, William." She wrenched the reins from his hands and urged her horse onward.

He allowed the reins to slip through his hands, giving her the ability to move forward. Her heart wrenched a little. It surprised her. She didn't know she was capable of feeling anything anymore.

She heard him mutter something under his breath before cantering ahead of her. There, he reined in his horse, forcing her to stop.

"I would have you listen to me, Alice de Courcy. You have known me long enough to consider me as something more than a mere acquaintance. Then, I had nothing to bring you, and I kept my distance. But now everything has changed. What I need to know now is what has wrought this change in you. Have your feelings toward me altered from what they were when you were a lass?"

Alice felt the blood surge to her cheeks. She'd never heard William speak so many words at one time, nor such important ones, nor ones which devastated her to the core. The world around her ceased to exist. Her usually vivid perceptions of everything bar sound focused on that one person. She allowed herself one lingering look at his face before she lied.

"That was a long time ago, William. I am a lass no more. Time has changed everything." It seems she couldn't bring herself to lie to him entirely.

"You did not answer my question."

She met his gaze steadily, waiting for her heart to harden. She took a deep breath. "Am I so hard to understand?"

"When you speak in riddles, yes. Tell me, have your feelings toward me changed?"

In the distance, she heard the thrum of horses' hooves. It would be the guards come looking for her. It was enough. "They have." There, the lie had been uttered.

His gaze narrowed and hardened, but he did not look away from her. Instead, he drew closer, and her breath snatched from her throat. He inclined his head toward her, watching her response, her flushed cheeks, and rising chest. "I never knew you to lie before, Alice. Something is amiss."

She shook her head. He must not become involved.

He pushed a stray lock behind her ear. "There's no point denying it." He glanced toward the approaching horsemen from the castle and settled back into his saddle. "I will talk with your mother this day and settle the matter."

She reached out to him in a panic. "No!" She shook her head. "You cannot."

"Give me one good reason why not."

"Because…" She hesitated. "Because, William, there is little point. My mother will not agree to a wedding between you and me." She avoided naming her guardian, who she knew William despised.

"Why not?" There was a sense of menace in his voice she hadn't heard before.

"Because she is not the woman she once was. She is ruled by…" She hesitated, but could no longer avoid naming him. "Sir Bayard. They wish me to marry someone else."

"Who?"

"I know not, truly."

"Then I shall call upon them before it is too late. So long as your feelings haven't changed toward me, Alice, then I shall ask for your hand. I won't let anything come between us now."

Her heart leaped and she forgot what had happened to her in the intervening years. Maybe she could persuade Bayard to have a change of heart about her marriage? Perhaps she could forget the damage which had been wrought to her body and soul in the last six years? She chewed her lip. With William beside her, she suddenly felt anything was possible.

"Come tomorrow. I will speak with them both."

William's brow eased, and the familiar warmth shot into

his eyes again. "If that is what you think best. I am content for now knowing what is in your heart."

She nodded as the familiar doubts and fears began to crowd at the back of her mind. "Aye. But…"

He took her hand and robbed her of her breath. "No buts, Alice. It is time."

Before she could speak, he pressed her hand to his lips. For one long moment, she was only aware of the heat of his lips sending flames of a long-dormant fire along her skin, and deeper inside of her to parts of her she never wished to think about.

Then he looked up at her with eyes much darker than usual, and flicked the reins of his horse to turn away.

She pressed the back of her hand against her flaming cheek, lost for words against this onslaught of feeling. He reined in his horse who danced beneath him, ready to speed away. "It is time, Alice," he repeated, before turning and cantering along the dusty lane, leaving her breathless with desire for him. But as soon as he'd gone, the familiar dread sized her once more.

It spread like ice over water, freezing her, turning her to stone for all the world to see. And making her believe, until this moment, that she was stone. But the dread deepened because now she knew she wasn't. And she also knew that that would only make everything so much worse than it already was.

CHAPTER 2

With her head held high, Alice allowed the groom to lead her horse into the castle bailey, deserted on that hot, sultry afternoon. It didn't matter that she was deaf in one ear—she could still hear her mother's anxious, pleading tones, followed by the hectoring voice of her father's cousin. Since her father's untimely death, his cousin, Sir Bayard of Wrotham, had reappeared, ingratiating himself with her mother, and taking control of their lives once more, claiming his role as Alice's guardian.

She dismounted and slid damp palms down her gown as she turned to face the castle. What had once been her home, had become a battleground of lust and greed. She hated the sight of it. She briefly bent to pet her favorite hound before summoning all her courage and stepping into the Hall.

Alice paused at the entrance, blinking to allow her eyes to adjust to the dark. Unlike Wanham Castle, her family's castle was antiquated, dark, and smoky. While it was far grander, it was also far less comfortable. But comfort had little meaning for the de Courcy family. All they wanted was power.

"You've deigned to come back from your wanderings, I see," Sir Bayard thundered at her. Alice ignored him and searched the gloom to see who else was in the Hall. She didn't see her at first, lost in the smoky room, half-hidden by the back of a chair. It was only when her mother turned her face up to Bayard that she saw her. Her heart wrenched to see her once proud mother turn pleading eyes upon him. Only then did Alice face the man she loathed.

"I haven't been wandering. I've been visiting the Priory, helping the sick."

He spat into the rushes. "The sick? You'd do better to pay attention to the sick here"—he indicated her mother—"than the poor." He brushed crumbs from his usually immaculate robes. "They'll do nothing for this family."

Alice twitched her skirts from being caught in the rushes and walked over to her mother. She placed a hand on her shoulder, and her mother briefly held her palm against hers before catching the eye of Bayard and withdrawing it. He didn't like signs of their affection. It drew the power away from him. United women would threaten him.

"Don't bother trying to look to your pathetic mother for help. She's leaving for the North on the morrow."

Alice felt the energy sap away from her mother beneath her hand.

"The North? But why?"

"I'm going to live with my brother in the Borders." Her mother cast a cowed and anxious glance at Bayard. "Sir Bayard deems it to be best."

"Best for whom?" Alice glared at Bayard.

But Bayard ignored her question. Instead, he beckoned the maid to him, who poured him yet another goblet of wine. From the looks of the red-stained rushes around him, it looked like Bayard had been drinking most of the afternoon.

He glared as she caught his eye, but she didn't look away and nor did he as he drank back the wine. He placed the goblet on the oak table with a bang, spilling the last few drops. He swept the back of his hand across his mouth.

"Did you hear me, girl?" he bellowed. "Or do I have to come over and speak in your good ear?" His lips curled into a grin.

"You do not," she said crisply, not wanting him anywhere near her. The hairs on the back of her dog's neck bristled, and she felt his low growl against her leg as he positioned himself between her and Bayard. "I hear you quite well enough."

Her mother shot her a somber look before returning to pleating her gown with agitated fingers. It hurt Alice to see her mother diminished by the schemes of this man.

"Then why do you not answer, girl?" He beckoned the maid for more wine. "I said," he repeated, "what do you intend to do for our family?"

Alice bit her lip and turned away. She couldn't bear to look at him; she couldn't bear knowing how much he used not only her but her mother and father, his own cousin. The thought of the havoc he'd wrought on her family made the anger that lay deep inside of her spark suddenly. She twisted her head and saw her anger reflected in his face. He looked momentarily shocked. It gave her the courage to continue.

"Our family? You do not belong to our family!"

"Alice," her mother pleaded.

Bayard strode over to her and stood too close. The smell of his body made the gorge rise in her throat. But she wouldn't shift her gaze this time.

"Why you little—" He slapped her face, and she spun around, her head buzzing.

She turned to face him again. "Are you trying to make me

deaf in the other ear, as you did before? Surely not? That would only weaken your prized possession, wouldn't it? You made that mistake once. Surely you do not intend to make it again?"

His fists clenched, and his face went white around his mouth, while his eyes were coal black. But he managed to restrain himself, for he knew that she spoke the truth.

He paced away before swinging around to face her. "The fact remains, girl, that you should have been here, readying yourself for your departure."

"Departure? To where? I know nothing of this." She turned to her mother. "What is this?"

Her mother didn't answer, but instead, she held her head in her hands.

Alice was forced to turn back to Bayard.

"If your mother won't tell you, I will. An arrangement has been reached. You are to marry Ralph de Gant."

Alice gasped and leaned against a chair. She knew he'd been up to something, but hadn't enquired, hadn't wanted to know, hadn't wanted to face up to his devious plans. All she'd heard of this man—Ralph de Gant—was that he was past middle age, unscrupulous, and coveted their lands. He also had influence at court.

"I will not!" She felt her face flush, unable to keep her usual composure. The anger gave her strength. "You may be able to make my mother do anything for you, but you will not make me!"

He laughed. "You have no choice, girl. You will marry Ralph de Gant. The Lord knows, no one else will have you. He wants the castle and lands."

"And what will it bring you?" For she knew that it would be Bayard who would profit most.

His cruel lips curled into a sickening smile that didn't

reach his eyes. "Plenty. I certainly won't have to hang around here with you de Courcy women anymore."

For a moment, Alice thought it would be worth marrying her family's enemy simply to rid her family of Bayard. But she'd met Ralph de Gant once before as a child, and had heard much more of him since. He was one such as Bayard. Marriage to him would be the end of her.

"Then I'm afraid you're in for a disappointment. I will *not* be marrying Ralph de Gant."

"Won't you now?" His voice was dangerous. He prowled around her like a hungry wolf, circling his prey. She shivered but refused to move. "Why, do you plan on marrying someone else?"

The vision of William filled her mind. She hadn't been able to give him a reason why he should not visit her mother and ask for Alice's hand. Instead, she'd given him hope. It was madness. She couldn't marry. She wanted only to call the Priory home. But that moment of madness when he'd held her hand had stopped her reply.

Suddenly Bayard lifted her chin and looked deeply into her eyes, his own eyes narrowing as if he could read her. She'd made a mistake; she'd forgotten to hide her thoughts.

"You do wish to marry. Who?"

She licked her lips as her mind raced, trying to find ways in which she could cover up her mistake. "I…"

His head tilted to one side, and he glanced at her mother. "It's not William de Vere, is it? Don't tell me he still harbors notions of claiming you?"

She shook her head, but she could feel a blush rising on her pale cheeks.

"He does!" He laughed and twisted her head before releasing her. "Well, he won't win you. We have a much bigger prize than him!"

Anger filled her at the thought that William wasn't a

prize. He was too big a prize for her. There was no way she could marry him because she felt too much for him. She knew what he wanted from life, and, equally, she knew that she couldn't give it to him. But watching Bayard insult William made her forget her intentions.

"William is the best man I know!" Heat pulsed across her cheeks. Even her mother had risen from her chair and was staring at her as if she didn't recognize her.

"If he wanted you, he'd have the balls to come to the castle and ask for your hand in marriage."

"He fully intends to."

"Well, he'll be out of luck. We'll be gone by the time he arrives. Or at least I'll make sure we're gone. When is he coming?"

Alice's mind raced. The instant she was taken from this castle, she'd be lost. William was her only means of rescue now. "The day after tomorrow."

"Two days? He cares little to rush, then! So be it. I'm in no mood to deal with him."

Alice knew that Bayard most certainly wouldn't want to deal with William. Bayard was a coward who always took the easy way out.

"We'll leave for Lincolnshire earlier than planned to avoid your William." He sighed as if affecting unconcern. "It doesn't pay to aggravate the de Veres. Avoidance is the best strategy."

Alice was relieved. She'd lied about when William was due. He'd arrive before she was taken away from Norfolk. He was an honorable man, and she knew that, even if she refused his marriage offer, he'd help her escape Bayard.

She lowered her lashes. She couldn't afford to allow Bayard to see into her mind again. "Whatever you say, sir. I think I'll retire now. I'm feeling a little unwell."

He waved her away. "Go then, girl."

. . .

ALICE STAYED in her bedchamber for the rest of that evening. She had only one night to avoid Bayard until William came. She could do that.

But as she closed the shutters on the starry night, her maid entered with an armful of winter clothes and opened a chest.

"What is it you're doing?" she asked her maid.

Her maid gave her a look of sympathy. "Readying your clothes for the journey to Lincolnshire on the morrow."

"Nay, the plan is for the day after tomorrow."

"I'm sorry, my lady. But Sir Bayard has changed those plans. He says you are to be ready for tomorrow morning —early."

"Then why did he not tell me?"

Her maid was silent. She half-turned away, and muttered something.

"What is it?"

Her maid looked up at her. "I think, my lady, that he did not want you to know."

Ice filled her veins. "Why?"

"I heard him say that he did not trust you. That he wanted to make sure you were gone before Sir William arrived."

Alice glanced toward the window. The night was dark, and the rain that had threatened all day now fell, bringing a chill to the air. She shivered. It was too late to do anything. She'd send William a message first thing. He had to come early on the morrow. Or else all would be lost.

WILLIAM ROSE BEFORE ALL the others. He always liked the early morning when there was nothing in his head except what he wanted—the peaceful, reassuring sounds of the birds overhead and the workers emerging into the fields. It was what he knew. It was what he wanted.

But this morning, there was something else he wanted, something which made him not even hear the usual squawk of cockerels or grunt of pigs as they were being led out into the fields.

He took his ale and walked to the gatehouse and looked east to where the sun was about to rise. How many mornings had he done this as a single man? But not for much longer. Soon he would have Alice by his side, and all would be well.

He cast a long glance around the sandbanks beyond which the sea lay, quiet this morning, but he was still aware of the underlying surge and pull of the sea on the sand. Some things you were born to know, born to live and die with, and the sea and the land were one of them, as was Alice. For many years he'd thought her above him, but since Rufus had given him the lands as his own, he felt, for the first time, that he had something to offer her. And since that time, each day that had passed had dragged. Today was the day for action.

He tossed the last bit of ale from his cup and returned to the Hall. Katherine was already talking with a messenger who he'd heard arrive while he'd been out on the road. He could tell from Katherine's pursed mouth that there was nothing good in what she was reading. But he didn't say anything. He rarely did. Katherine would tell him if he should know.

She looked up at him suddenly. "Are you still planning to ride over to the de Courcy castle this morning?"

He wondered how she knew. But then Katherine seemed to know everything that was going on. "Aye. I told Alice I would, and so I shall."

"Could you forestall your visit by a day?"

He shook his head as he shrugged on his mantle. "Nay,

Kat. I don't wish to do that. It's been long enough already, and I told her I would come."

She sighed, and her brow furrowed. He tried to ignore it, but she looked at him again with those big brown eyes, which were usually so patient and loving but in which all he could see now was concern.

"Why, what is it? What's happened?"

"The new captain of the Yarmouth Princess won't agree to take the shipment of herrings to Bordeaux. He says whatever the previous captain had agreed is null and void, and he insists on a new agreement."

"Then why do you not make one? You have Mother's paperwork. You've done such negotiations before."

Her brown eyes flashed darker. "Because"—she waved the paperwork—"he refuses to do business with a woman!"

William shook his head. "If Mother were alive, she'd have something to say about that!"

"But she's not." Katherine's voice had lowered and had become controlled to hide the pain that was still raw at their mother's death. "And I am not her. I can run things, I can administer things, but men such as these talk over me, they refuse to listen to me. They rob me of my power."

"Look at me, Katherine," he said, stepping toward her, and put his hands on her shoulders. She looked up trustingly into his eyes. "You are as strong as Mother."

"I know that. Unfortunately, Captain James Logan does not. You have to go and convince him, William. He'll listen to a man."

And he knew it. These seagoing men only understood one thing—strength. And for all Katherine's sense, goodness and abilities, these tough men would ride rough-shod over her.

"There's a lot at stake, William. Not only this cargo, but for the next few years, also."

"I'll go. But it will have to be tomorrow. I cannot go before then."

"Tomorrow will not do. It'll be too late by then. There's already another merchant ready to supply if we don't convince the captain to honor the agreement Mother made with the previous captain." She paused and shook her head, her whole body tense. "It has to be today, William. No later."

He nodded slowly. His future would have to wait. Alice would have to wait. One more day. What could one more day matter when he'd been waiting so many years?

"I'll go. I'll send a message to Alice and let her know I'll be late."

WILLIAM'S HORSE'S hooves pounded the soft ground as he rode as hard as he could from Yarmouth, direct to the de Courcy castle. The morning's meeting with the difficult captain had gone well, of that he was assured, which would mean prosperity. But he was less comfortable about having not gone to Alice when he'd arranged. He was a man of his word, and when he found that his messenger had not delivered his message direct to Alice, it had worried him.

Despite his swift pace, it was dark when he arrived at the castle. He jumped off his horse, and the steward emerged. They greeted each other.

"You've come a long way, this cold night, Sir William!"

"Aye. I'm here to visit Lady de Courcy. She'll be expecting me."

The steward looked uncomfortable. "She is not here, I'm afraid. Gone to her brother in the Border country."

"Gone?" William frowned. "Then I shall see Lady Alice." The thought of seeing her alone was enticing.

"Lady Alice is gone, also."

"Where to?"

There was an awkward pause during which it seemed the steward was trying to decide what to say.

"Lincolnshire."

William shook his head in bewilderment, his stomach sinking like a stone. "Why, in God's name?"

The steward licked his lips and swallowed. "To be wed. To Sir Ralph de Gant."

CHAPTER 3

William paced the floor while Katherine watched.

"It's fine," she repeated. "Besides, Savari is expected any day. He'll be here with us. And then there's our steward, Sir Harry, as well as our neighbors. We need no further care. All will be well."

William looked at his resourceful sister and briefly believed her. But then he sighed and pushed his hands through his hair. "I can't leave you alone. I can't go to..." His voice nearly broke as he was about to say Alice's name.

He felt a hand on his arm. "You can, and you must. If it is as you say and Alice has been taken by force to Lincolnshire to the de Gants, she needs you, William. You must bring her home. She cannot marry Ralph de Gant. I've heard nothing but ill of him."

Ill. William tested the word in his mouth, and he tasted nothing but evil. He nodded and glanced once more at Katherine. "I will take only one man with me."

Katherine nodded. She didn't question William as to

whether he needed to take anyone else. She knew him better than that. "If you are sure."

"I am. I need no one else to help me bring her home."

"When will you leave?"

"I cannot wait for Savari. I'll leave immediately."

"Good." Katherine turned to the window to look north, in the direction where Alice had been taken. "I cannot bear to think of her at the mercy of Ralph de Gant."

William walked toward the door as his man hurried after him with all that he would need. He only had one thought on his mind. Alice. He had to get her before Ralph could do her harm.

IT WAS the second day since Alice had arrived in Lincolnshire. The journey north had been hurried, and Bayard had wasted no time in getting to the de Gant stronghold. And stronghold it was, she thought, as she twisted around and swept her gaze around the forbidding gray stone walls which sat on the flat landscape like a warning. A warning she didn't need.

She'd only managed to escape outside because her maid had taken the eye of one of the men guarding her room. But even with her maid's help, she wouldn't have been able to slip away if Bayard hadn't already left for the King's Court.

Immediately upon delivering Alice to Ralph de Gant, Bayard had been sent away. Not that he cared. He'd got what he'd wanted from Ralph and was eager to see which of the sought-after roles the King would give him. Whichever one, it would mean a life of power and privilege, and he was keen to begin it. While Alice was thankful to see the back of him, she now had a new enemy in Ralph, whose character seemed little improved on Bayard's.

So she grasped the rare opportunity and ran swiftly

through the long grass toward the trees, which marked the edge of the woods through which the road south ran. It would be along this road that William would come.

How she knew he'd come, she could not have said. She'd dreamed of it, for sure. But then she'd dreamed of many things which hadn't come to pass. Truth was, she knew him. She knew how he'd react, and that he would come after her. She knew this like she knew that rain would fall from dull leaden clouds and that from the earth, green shoots would rise without fail after the frosts had passed. William was like the land and skies around her—unfailing and dependable.

She didn't have to wait long. She felt the thudding in the soil before she heard it. She stepped into the middle of the path. Despite her predicament, her blood raced at the thought of seeing William again.

He and his squire came around the long corner, and she saw in the set of his shoulders the instant he recognized her. He slowed his horse and leaped to his feet. He reached out to her briefly before dropping his arms to his sides.

"Alice! Are you hurt? Why do you stand here?"

"To see you, of course."

He shook his head. "You knew." A smile flickered on his lips. She could see he was pleased, believing no doubt that she trusted him to come. But trust had nothing to do with it. She trusted no one, not anymore. She simply knew him.

She nodded. "I knew you'd come. And I had to stop you."

His travel-begrimed face creased into a frown. "Stop? You know nothing would stop me from getting to you." This time he did not prevent his hands gripping her shoulders. "You are safe now."

She wanted to be. Oh, how much she wanted to feel safe, with William. But she knew that such a feeling would be temporary only and that it would result in danger for them all, and ultimately unhappiness. He mistook her silence for agreement. She glanced at the castle. They'd be looking for her by now.

"Tell me what has happened."

"Sir Bayard brought me to this detestable place two days ago. He and Ralph de Gant have come to an arrangement, so it seems. I am given to de Gant, and, in return, Sir Bayard receives riches and favor at court, where he is now."

"It will not happen." He spoke each word with emphasis. "Come. Come away with me now. We need not go to the castle if you desire." He glanced up at it with a black look. "Although I would like to go and deal with Ralph de Gant personally."

She laid her hand upon his chest, her fingers smoothing over the sturdy wool of his cloak. "No! You must not. He is a ruthless man."

"And so am I, if anyone tries to hurt you."

"He will not hurt me. I am too valuable. Now, anyway." She couldn't help thinking of the time when her only brother had been alive, and her value had been less, and Bayard had hurt her.

William's eyebrows beetled together. "What do you mean?"

She shook her head. She'd vowed never to tell William even a part of what had happened over the years between her innocence and now. "It is of no import. What is of import is that you must leave. You cannot enter the castle. I've heard Bayard and Ralph speak. They are closely allied with Gilbert de Montmorency's son and have pledged to help him avenge Sir Gilbert's death."

"Rufus killed him after he'd killed our mother. Gilbert de Montmorency deserved everything that was coming to him.
"

"I don't doubt it. His son is cut from the same cloth and is demanding support from his allies." She couldn't prevent a shiver from tracking down her spine. She looked into William's eyes. "They want your blood. You must *not* come to the castle."

"He will not have my blood, Alice. I can look after myself."

She glanced at his only companion. "You are but two. They are many. You must leave, William." Her throat clenched with fear and emotion. "William, please, you must do this… for me."

"For you?" It was the only thing she'd said that he'd listened to. She pressed her advantage.

"Yes. You are outnumbered there. What can we do if you are captured?" She pressed her finger against his lips before he could begin to remonstrate. "We would both be imprisoned. We would be worse off than before."

"I will leave on one condition. That you come with me now."

When she opened her mouth, she didn't know what was going to emerge. Would it be a word, one word, that would rise on the wave of her feelings, feelings that she didn't ever dare acknowledge? Or would it be another word, an opposite word, arrived at by careful consideration of what had happened to her, and what she knew of this beloved man, and what he wanted? She knew her urge to agree to his condition was on the tip of her tongue. And, equally, she knew she must not allow her heart to rule her head.

Her head shook first, and then she felt the strength of the second word emerge. "No. I cannot."

"Cannot? Why? Do you need to collect your things?"

She shook her head. "I have nothing I value here."

"Then, why?"

"Because there is no time to prepare. I gained a few minutes to come here to warn you, but they will come looking for me soon. And they will find us. I cannot come with you now, William, because *they* have the advantage, not us."

He was silent as he considered her words and then nodded. "You speak truly, although I would risk it if you were prepared to."

"You risk too much." She glanced behind her, anxious that she'd been followed, before turning back to him. "You risk yourself, and that I cannot agree to."

Suddenly she heard the wrenching of the drawbridge as it was lowered, and she knew that her absence had been noted. She pulled her hands from his large ones which, although strong, allowed her fingers to slip through. She gave a brief smile at the difference between William and the other men who'd forced themselves into her life.

"They are coming for me. And when they find me, they must not find you, for it is Ralph's desire to see you dead."

"How can I let you return to that castle, Alice? You will be entirely at their mercy."

"I will be at their mercy if you come, William. For you will be dead and of no help to me, or your sisters." The truth was, she had no thought for herself or William's sisters. For if he was dead, so would she be, in her heart.

The thudding of the horse's hooves grew louder. "Go." She held her breath. He took one step back, and she released it. "Go," she repeated. "If you feel anything for me, please go. I will be safe." He took another step and turned and spoke briefly to his squire, and within seconds they were both lost from sight in the thick forest. No trace survived of them on the hard, frosty ground.

She turned to face the small posse of horses which was coming to find her. As they came around the bend into sight, they slowed at the sight of her. To her relief, they didn't look beyond her, or into the woods. Even if they did, she knew William and his squire wouldn't be seen. They were too clever for that. Despite that, she had to fight an urge to look to where she'd last seen William. To retain a small piece of their recent contact, which would get her through the forthcoming meeting. For she'd lied to William. She knew she wouldn't be safe. But if that was the price for securing his future, so be it.

WILLIAM and his squire led the two horses away from the road but stopped while Alice was still in sight. He'd retreated because she'd spoken sense. He'd heard the number of horses approaching, and he'd known he hadn't stood a chance if they were really against him, as Alice had said.

When he'd first thought to rescue Alice, he'd had no notion that he wouldn't succeed. He'd reasoned that Bayard would see sense in allowing her to come with him. After all, Bayard was Alice's kin, so surely he'd want her to be happy? What he hadn't factored into the equation was Bayard's greed, which had seen him depart for King John's court immediately, leaving Alice alone and unprotected, at the mercy of a man who, it appeared, wanted his blood.

No, Ralph would see him dead before allowing him to walk into the castle and take Alice away.

What he needed was something Savari would find easy. What he needed was a plan.

"THERE'S a traveler staying the night. A stranger." Alice's maid momentarily stopped brushing her hair. "He's handsome."

Alice thought she meant William—the only man who she considered to be handsome. "What does he look like?"

"Straight, fair hair and the face of an angel."

The small light of hope which had bubbled up inside of

Alice burst abruptly. Even people who loved William would never have described him as having the face of an angel. She sighed.

"He has a lute. He wants everyone to come and listen. Will you come, my lady? He especially asked about you. And, besides, it will ensure the men keep away. They cannot abide the minstrels. They'll never know you've left your chamber."

Alice hadn't intended to. But anything to ensure distance between herself and Ralph de Gant. "Aye. I'll come." Besides, she needed something to distract her thoughts from William. He'd gone. She'd sent him away. And there was nothing she could do about that.

Her maid helped Alice ready herself. Since the men had found her outside the castle walls, she'd been told to keep to her chambers. They seemed to accept the fact that she'd been picking rare herbs as a reason for her being outside the walls. It had been a stroke of luck that she'd been able to use the herbs to help one of the soldiers with a skin complaint.

She slipped past the sleeping soldier, drunk from too much wine plied on him by the maid, and went toward the music she could hear coming from the Hall. The fire was roaring, and people were dancing. The men had gathered upstairs in the solar, no doubt discussing the finer points of dividing Alice's inheritance between them.

"Come, my lady," said her maid. "Think not of what awaits. For tonight enjoy the music and wine. Lying upstairs, worrying, will not make things better for the morning."

Within moments she was seated in the shadows at the back of the room, and wine and food was being pressed on her. She was grateful for the help of these people who served the de Gants. They'd born witness to her indignity, and she'd helped some of them within the last few days to ease their ailments. She'd found loyalty in their hearts for her, where none existed for their cruel overlord.

As the dancers moved, she saw who it was playing the harp. Her mouth went dry. It was Warin, William's man. She gave a jump of surprise and spilled some wine. Then she sat back and gripped the cup, thankful that no one could see the flush that rose in her cheeks as her mind raced.

He hadn't left. William hadn't left. Instead, he'd sent his man to entertain and distract the others. Why?

Another song struck up, and Warin began to wander around the Hall, singing to people. He stopped beside her, sang a song, and bowed deeply. When he was finished, he leaned forward while the others stopped dancing and caught their breath.

"My lady, my lord will be waiting at the postern gate for you after the lights in the chambers are extinguished."

"But how?"

Warin smiled. "It seems you have already made friends here." He glanced at her maid, who smiled back. There was a sound outside, as men spilled down from the chamber overhead. Business had obviously been completed. Thankfully no one looked over to her. She was a pawn, but an invisible one to them all.

She nodded to Warin. "I'll be there as soon as I can after Sir Ralph has retired for the night."

"As soon as you can, my lady." He glanced at the men. "Every moment my lord waits is dangerous to him. And to you." He bowed and was soon lost amid people eager for more songs.

Alice looked around, assessing the danger before seating herself once more. It was best not to draw attention to herself. She'd remain in the shadows, unnoticed as yet by the men, and she'd watch them. She looked at Ralph de Gant, whose narrow eyes glittered under the billowing torchlight in the drafty castle. She'd follow his every movement and slip away as soon as she could.

Every moment is dangerous to him. Warin's words repeated in her mind. Then she had an idea. She beckoned over her maid and whispered her plan. Her maid nodded and slipped away, unnoticed, up to Alice's bedchamber. When she re-emerged wearing Alice's demure, plain robes, Alice's heart quickened. From a distance, her maid looked exactly like her.

By the time her maid was seated in Alice's place, her face in the shadows, her gown concealing her maid's more buxom figure, Alice was gone, running quietly through the kitchen and the passages which led to the outbuildings and then to the postern gate.

She paused at the end of the passage. Across the short width of courtyard lay the door. She waited until her eyes adjusted to the darkness. All was silent. Everyone was in the Hall listening to Warin's music, as William intended. Was he there?

She wasn't sure, but then she saw him. His dark cloak, a shade lighter than the dark stone wall behind him. He held out his hand into the light, and any doubt fled. She lifted her skirts and ran across the courtyard toward him and fell into his arms.

He put his arms around her and held her tight against him. She'd never been so physically close to him. The air was pushed from her lungs, and tears sprung to her eyes in relief.

"Oh, William, you came back."

He held her shoulders between firm hands. "Aye. Of course. Why wouldn't I?"

She huffed a brief laugh. "Because I told you to go?" she ventured.

"I heed you when you speak truly, Alice." His eyes ranged over her face, and he swept away a lock of her hair from her cheek. "But not then. I could not leave you at his mercy. I will take you far from here. And then it is up to you to decide what you wish to happen. I lay no claim to you."

She nodded and pressed her cheek against his chest, and he held her there, clasped close. Then he pulled away.

"We cannot tarry. We must go now."

She nodded and swept her cheeks with the flat of her hand. "Of course. I'm ready."

"My horse is tethered not too far away."

"And Warin?"

"He will follow."

He took her hand, looked around, and quietly opened the postern gate. The reason for its lack of guard was immediately evident. Two men lay tied up, unnoticed, within the wall. She gasped.

"Come."

She did not need telling twice and was about to step out and follow William into the darkness when lights flared all around them. They found themselves surrounded by a small cordon of men, at the center of which was Ralph de Gant.

"Going for a late-night stroll with my betrothed, Sir William?" Sir Ralph unsheathed his sword and stepped forward. "I think not."

CHAPTER 4

Ralph's men forced Alice and William back inside the castle, through a now deserted Hall and up to the solar.

"Take a seat, Sir William," said Ralph.

"Nay. I'd rather stand."

One of the guards tried to make Alice sit on a chair, wresting her arm behind her back, making her squeal with pain. She bit his arm, and the guard lifted his hand to strike her. William stepped between them and gripped the upraised hand, twisting it until the guard yelped with pain.

"You," said William, his anger palpable, "will never touch Lady Alice again."

Ralph stepped forward. "Release him, Sir William."

"I will not. He will strike the lady."

"No, he won't," Ralph said steadily. "Do you wish to know why?" But Ralph did not await an answer. No doubt he knew what it would be. "Because I will make sure of it. No one will strike my betrothed."

William considered his words, and then flicked away the guard, inflicting more pain as he released him. The guard fell to the floor, nursing his arm and cursing William.

Ralph looked behind him, and two guards moved forward and took hold of William and held him fast.

"No one that is," said Ralph, approaching Alice, "except me."

Before Alice or William could react, Ralph cast a stinging blow on Alice's cheek. It made her head ring, and she could feel blood trickle from her lip. But she stood tall and stared at Ralph, allowing the hate to show in her usually impassive face.

William roared impotently beside her. He caught her eye above the others, and she tried to reassure him. They quieted each other and, despite the roar, he conveyed a sense of hope and reassurance simply by his presence.

"Leave her alone," bellowed William.

Ralph tilted his head to one side. "Or what?" He approached William, who was now held firmly by two of his men. Ralph threw up his hands in mock fright. "You'll take me down? I hardly think you're in a position to issue commands or threats." He taunted William with his expression, before turning to his men who laughed along with him. "No," he said slowly, before turning his back on William and stepping toward Alice once more. He picked up a lock of her hair and pulled it between his fingers. Alice refused to utter any sound despite the pain. "She is mine to do with as I like."

"She's not yours."

Ralph didn't even bother to turn back to William. "Not yet. But she will be."

He made an elaborate bow to Alice. "Come, Lady Alice, take a seat."

She glanced at William, who nodded. Did he have a plan? Or did he simply want her to agree so as not to provoke Ralph again? She did not know but took her seat beside

Ralph. Sharp regret stung her mouth. She should have gone with William when she had the chance. Instead, she'd brought him here where anything could happen to him, and probably would. *She'd* done this. She'd brought this on the man who meant most to her in the world. And she knew that if the chance arose, she'd have no qualms in joining him now. She had to find a way for them to escape. She owed it to William.

Ralph took a seat beside her and indicated to William's captors that they should bring him forward. They tied him to a chair. After he was secured, Ralph dismissed his men.

Alice's hopes lifted. Ralph was underestimating William. She saw William flex his muscles against the bindings.

"What do you hope to gain from marriage to Lady Alice?" asked William.

"Hope? I need no hope. I can tell you what I'll gain. I'll have the de Courcy castle and lands which I have long coveted. And I'll have put one over you, which my friends the de Montmorencys will appreciate as your brother, Rufus, murdered their father."

"Aye, and he deserved everything he had coming to him."

Alice gasped as Ralph slammed a fist into William's mouth. William turned and spat blood into the already soiled rushes. Ralph stepped back, shaking his hand as if he hadn't anticipated how much the blow would hurt him. "Keep quiet, man."

Alice could feel the primitive growl William emitted. She jumped up and turned to Ralph, taking William's earlier lead. "If it's wealth you want, take it. But don't take me."

Ralph looked from one to the other of them. "You want to go with William? You wish to wed him?"

She looked at William, who nodded encouragement. But she couldn't lie. She turned back to Ralph, not wanting to see William's reaction to her words. "I wish to marry no one."

Ralph laughed and repeated her words in a high voice, mimicking her. "And who cares what you wish for?"

"If it's my lands you want," persisted Alice, "I will make them over to you. My mother has relinquished any rights in return for her dower lands. The lands are mine to give, and I will give you what I have if, in return, I am allowed to go free."

Ralph was tempted. Alice could see that, but then he turned to William, and a different light lit his eyes. "It *was* what I wanted. But not now. Sir William's presence has given me a better idea."

He pulled up his chair, so he was seated in front of William, and if it hadn't been for William being tied to the chair, it would have looked as if they were in earnest discussion.

"Tell me," said William in a deep threatening voice.

"What say you to leaving here this evening with the Lady Alice?"

William nodded.

Ralph pretended he didn't understand. "I'm sorry?" He cupped his hand around his ear as if to hear better. "What did you say?"

"That," ground out William, "is my intention."

Ralph sat back, pretending to be satisfied. "Then, you can. Go. Both of you."

Alice and William exchanged looks. It could not be that easy.

"No conditions?"

Ralph shrugged. "There *wasn't* going to be one." Alice knew that he was lying; that he was playing with them both. There was always going to be a condition. "But now you mention it, I will give you one." He looked from one to the other. William's eyes were dark and narrow.

"What is it?" William growled. "What is your condition?"

Ralph no longer pretended he had any interest in Alice. His attention was focused on William. "You can have Alice. If..." His lips tweaked at their corners, and Alice could feel Ralph's self-satisfaction. "If you give me *your* lands." Ralph rose, his blood heated by this new idea. "Yes, your lands. The de Vere lands. Wanham Castle and all the de Vere estates. You give them all to me, and you can have Alice." He stepped back, triumphant. "What say you?"

William ground his teeth and looked at Alice, then back at Ralph. "It is done."

Alice gasped. "No, William. You cannot."

William didn't turn to look at her but simply repeated. "It is done."

Only Alice knew what the lands meant to him, and she couldn't bear to see him thus tortured. "I don't wish to marry William. I will *not* marry William."

For the first time, Ralph looked at Alice and frowned. "You will not marry him?" He walked closer to her and raised his hand. She heard William growl again and struggle with his bindings. She didn't move but closed her eyes briefly. When she opened them again, Ralph's hand was still raised, and his mouth had curled into a smile. He liked to see her frightened. She vowed never to allow that to happen again.

"I will not marry him," she repeated. She daren't look at William.

"You *will* marry me, Alice," said William. She looked at him and shook her head.

"No, I cannot."

"Think of the alternative, Alice." She could hear the pleading in his voice.

She looked at Ralph. He might be past middle age, but he was big, strong, and cruel.

Suddenly the door opened, and a tall, handsome young man entered the solar. He strode in, his brow furrowed as he looked around. He came and stood beside Ralph. "What is this, father? What's afoot?"

It was the younger son, Adam, to whom Lora had been briefly affianced.

"Nothing to concern you, Adam."

Adam opened his mouth to speak but evidently thought better of it.

"Go, and take the guards with you. I'm about to teach them both a lesson."

Adam hesitated and gave William a long hard look and then a softer one at Alice.

"Then I will stay."

"No, you will not. Take the guards and leave."

Alice hoped that Adam would stay. She sensed in him a decency which was entirely lacking in his father. Adam tore his uncomfortable gaze from his father, settled briefly on Alice, and then left the room, followed by the guards.

Ralph turned to Alice.

"You will marry William because I want—not only your lands—but the de Vere lands." He grunted a laugh as he glanced at William. "I had not thought your lands would be surrendered so easily, Sir William." He turned back to Alice. "The fool must be in love with you." He huffed another, sinister laugh. "I wonder why." He tilted Alice's face first one way and then another. "You are certainly beautiful in a chilly kind of way."

Alice struggled to be free of his hand, but Ralph's grip slipped and went around her throat. Suddenly she found it hard to breathe.

"Leave her be!" William roared.

But Ralph didn't bother to respond. Instead his hand gripped her behind. "I think I'll try you out first. Put a de Gant brat in your belly and allow William to watch."

Alice struggled, and Ralph withdrew a knife and held it

against her throat. "I suggest you don't struggle. It'll go better for you that way."

Alice tried to cry out but received another slap for her trouble before Ralph tore the front of her gown. She struggled against him, feeling the cold blade of the knife slice into her neck and a trickle of warm blood descend her throat, onto her exposed neck, pooling between her breasts. She twisted away and looked straight into William's eyes.

With a silent roar William rose, twisted his hands in their loosened bindings, and brought the table crashing down on Ralph, freeing him from his bonds and sending Alice flying across the room. She sat up in a daze, holding her head, which had banged against the wooden floor, hardly buffered by the scanty rushes. She saw William fighting Ralph. Ralph had the knife poised above William's eye, but in one swift move, he'd overturned Ralph.

Ralph lay on the floor with his arms splayed either side in a gesture of submission. He glanced at the door, but his guards and son had taken him at his word and had left them quite alone, and hadn't heard the fight.

"You win, William. Back off now, and we'll forget this little episode."

William didn't move. He still brandished the knife at Ralph. "Why should I trust you?"

Ralph raised himself carefully, his eyes never leaving William's. "Why? Because you are an honorable man, are you not? And I say to you that I promise to honor your lady and abide by your wishes. There. From one honorable man to another." He held out his hand as if he wished to be helped up.

"No, William," said Alice. She'd learned that honor was rare and trust even rarer. She trusted no one. Particularly not Ralph de Gant. "You cannot trust him."

"I either trust him, Alice, or kill him." He placed the blade on the table. "And I'm in no mood for killing."

Alice groaned as she watched Ralph rise. She knew Ralph was not honorable, and as the men eyed each other warily, Alice stepped unnoticed to the table where the blade lay.

"Ah, you are truly a man of honor," said Ralph, standing up, his hands on his hips, surveying William.

"And now you must prove to me that *you* are also a man of honor," said William, his brow lowered, his eyes narrowed and fixed on Ralph. The slight flicker around Ralph's lips made Alice move more quickly toward the knife. William was strong and reliable, and he was honorable and loyal. Alice knew these things like she knew herself. She also knew where William's weakness lay. He believed the best in people. Lucky that she believed the worst.

"And how might I do that?" asked Ralph.

"Allow Alice to leave here, now, with me. Lay no further claim to her lands, or to mine."

Ralph grunted in grim amusement, and William's eyes narrowed further. "Anything else? Would you care for me to lie down and let you fuck me?"

William tilted his head to one side and then made the mistake of looking at Alice, who had made the most of the intense exchange by crouching by the table. One swift movement and the knife would be hers. It came sooner than she imagined.

Ralph launched himself at William, as William was still looking at Alice. With a cry, she leaped up, grabbed the knife, and threw herself on Ralph, thrusting the blade into Ralph's arm as he grasped William around the throat. She withdrew it quickly.

With a roar of pain, Ralph released his grip on William, and for the first time, Alice noticed Ralph had another knife on him. William and Ralph struggled on the floor. Ralph had his knife over William once more, and Alice screamed.

Immediately the door burst open, and Ralph's son, Adam, leaped in the room, closely followed, much to Alice's relief, by Warin, who, with one quick movement, tossed William a dagger while deftly holding another to Adam's throat.

Ralph roared and he and William thrashed briefly before becoming suddenly still.

Silence hung heavy in the air. It was Adam who broke the eerie quiet first. "Father!"

At the same time, Alice called William's name. For one long moment, she thought they were both dead. She cried out and rushed to them. She put her arm over William, and he gave a deep, shuddering breath and turned to her. Blood was spattered over his face, but he was alive and breathing. He rose and took her away from the man that was once Ralph de Gant, who now lay lifeless on the wooden floor in a pool of blood.

Adam struggled in Warin's arms.

"Let him go," William said to Warin. "He can do no harm. He is but a boy."

Warin released Adam, who staggered across the floor and crouched by his father. Alice thought she heard a sob, but when Adam turned to face William, hatred was the only emotion showing on his face. He spat at William.

"Even a boy can kill."

"Not without a weapon, lad," said Warin with a laugh.

"And boys can get weapons, and boys can grow." Adam rose and Alice suddenly felt frightened for William. "I will come for you and your family, and you will know the pain of loss."

"Too late, lad. I know that well enough already." William turned to Warin. "The others?"

"I've dealt with them."

William nodded. "Good. We'll tie this lad up, and then we'll leave." He turned to Alice. "Are you ready?"

Alice nodded and ran and retrieved her fur-lined cloak. When she returned, Ralph lay as William had left him, and Adam was bound and gagged beside him, his eyes shooting daggers.

Without a backward glance, the three of them slipped into the rear of the castle and out through the postern gate and into the dark wood before anyone could sound the alarm. There they found their horses and were soon galloping through the night.

Alice's last glimpse of the castle was its ominous outline, stark against the moonlit sky. She looked ahead once more, William's arms tight around her as if he'd never let her go.

The thunder of the horse's hooves resounded through her body, driving home to her the horror that they'd left behind. What had they done? She felt safe within William's arms, but for how long? Because, whether William knew it or not, she'd meant what she'd said to Ralph about not marrying William. And she felt its truth deep in her soul even more now. Because he'd killed for her, and she owed him everything. If she married him, she'd be robbing him of a future he desired beyond everything—a loving wife and family. And she couldn't do that to him.

CHAPTER 5

The ride passed in a blur of freezing wind, which made Alice's eyes water, and her body slowly stiffen as she held onto the saddle, cradled in William's arms.

From time to time, she'd glance at his face, which looked steadily ahead, eyes narrowed against the cold, mouth grim, and shadowed in the gray starlight, like a stone carving. Like someone she didn't know. A stranger. In those moments, she'd close her eyes hard but, still, the memory of William killing Ralph filled her mind. Then she'd open her eyes once more and focus on the unvarying landscape—mile after mile of flat land punctuated by poor dwellings huddled atop the few raised islands in the boggy landscape. At least the bleak land was better than the terrors of her mind.

Still they carried on, their horses pounding along the only road through that most northerly part of The Wash, aptly named for the vast water-logged land which divided Lincolnshire from Norfolk. The road was slightly raised, and, as the moon rose further, the silver light cast its uncanny sheen over the watery fields and meres, shedding more light upon them, making them more of a target.

Eventually, they came to a small village built around a wide-spanned bridge and, after a quick exchange with Warin, they led their horses into a nearby inn.

While Warin roused the innkeeper, William helped Alice from the horse. She felt frozen to the bone, and her body was awkward as she slipped to her feet, stumbling before William caught her in strong arms. But her mind was playing tricks on her, and she had the feeling that he was a stranger.

William frowned and called Warin over, who took the horses and led them into the stables.

"We will be safe here?" she asked.

"As safe as we can be. But we must stop for the horses. A few hours rest, and we'll be on our way again. But there's no sign of anyone following us."

"There's only one room free," said the old innkeeper, eyeing Alice carefully. "We're the only inn for miles around here," he added by way of explanation.

He didn't need to. It would also account for the soiled rushes and rough furniture. Alice tried to contain a shudder at the thought of the bed. But one look at William's gray face decided her. "We'll take it," she said.

"All three of you in the room?" The man's shaggy white brows raised in surprise.

"Aye," said Alice. "The men are exhausted."

"Nay, Alice. The room will be for you." William looked as shocked at the innkeeper.

"No," she said firmly. "We all need to sleep, and the taproom is too crowded."

"I can place a pallet for your man if you like?"

"Two pallets," said William firmly.

They followed the innkeeper up the stairs, as he barked out instructions to a sleepy lad who he'd awoken from before the fire.

Warin dropped the saddlebags on the floor, flopped down on the pallet, and immediately fell asleep.

Alice sat on the bed, suddenly more awake than she had been, warmed by the heat from the downstairs fire which filtered up into the top-most rooms. Suddenly William looked less of a stranger and, here, in the intimacy of this room, the thought wasn't comforting.

They held each other's gaze for one long, awkward moment before William turned away and lay on the pallet. It was too short for him by far.

"William," she said hesitantly. "Please, there is plenty of room on this bed. Lie here and sleep."

"Nay, it would not be right."

She huffed a laugh. "And what is right in our lives? We've killed a man and are on the run. No, I think lying beside me to sleep is the least of our worries."

He gave what passed for a smile and lay beside her, the bed creaking as his large frame lay on it. He left a space between them in which Warin could easily have fit.

She lay, unmoving, looking at the ceiling where the thatch was disturbed, and she could hear the sound of rats moving. "What have we done, William?" she asked softly. "What have we done?"

"*You* haven't done anything, Alice. Nothing. You're an innocent in all of this. And you're safe now."

She looked at him. "Do you truly believe that?"

He opened his mouth to speak, but no words emerged. She knew what that meant. Instead, he took her hand and squeezed it. "Get some sleep. Things will look better in the light of day. And we'll soon be home, and everything will be back to normal."

"Normal? I hope not," she whispered.

He touched her shoulder, and she turned to him. In the

gloom all she could see were his eyes, dark and intense with a longing he rarely showed.

"I don't know what happened to you, Alice, but I promise you will never have to suffer again. I'll make sure of that."

"But how can you, William?"

"Because I will make sure you don't leave my side ever again. I will protect you; I will honor you."

A shiver ran down Alice's back, whether from proximity to William or from fear, she couldn't tell. The feeling settled in her gut. She swallowed.

"Don't," she said, laying a hand on his arm. "Please don't."

"You won't leave my side," he repeated, ignoring her plea.

The unease in her gut strengthened. She shook her head. He seemed to interpret that as indecision.

"Don't worry, Alice. I will take you back to Wanham Castle and keep you by my side. No one will be able to get you there. All will be well, you'll see."

Suddenly a look of exhaustion took hold of him, and he kissed her on the forehead and then lay back and fell into a deep sleep. But Alice didn't. His words continued to ring in her ears. He thought he was being reassuring by telling her that he intended to control her. He thought he was helping her. What he didn't realize was that his words had struck a chord of terror deep inside of her that she couldn't contain. Because the last thing she wanted was to be kept in place by a man. The instinct of revolt that his words inspired, warred with her feelings for William. But ultimately, it won. She could not do as William said.

WILLIAM DIDN'T HAVE the heart to rouse Alice, who lay sleeping soundly. It didn't look as if she'd moved, which wasn't surprising given the events of the day before. No, he'd leave her sleeping while he arranged some food and made the final arrangements to leave.

Warin had already left the chamber, and William could hear his voice downstairs in the taproom, no doubt already tasting the goodwife's ale. He stepped heavily down the stairs, his heart full of Alice, his mind full of the man he'd killed the day before. The only witness had been Ralph's son, Adam. It would be his word against William's. And he had no idea whose word held the greatest sway with the King, should it get that far.

William greeted Warin and accepted a cup of ale, and ordered breakfast to be taken up to Alice.

Outside, the mist was curling around the outbuildings, rising from the fields. He sniffed the air. It would be a fair day, a good day for riding. With any luck, they'd reach Norwich, where they could spend the night at the house his brother, Savari, kept there. And he could talk to Savari about how best to proceed. And then they'd press on to Wanham. Simply the thought of his beloved lands and home brought him a deep-rooted sense of comfort. Alice would fit right in with his sisters, who loved her as if she were a sister. And with him. It was what was meant to be.

WILLIAM HAD BEEN RIGHT, things did seem better in the cold light of day. There was little time or energy to speak as they cantered at a brisk pace along the back roads toward Norwich. Compared to the desolate, flat, black lands of Lincolnshire, the lush undulating countryside around central Norfolk was like a balm to their inflamed spirits. It was the land she knew best and loved most. The damp cold of the Fens had been replaced by the drier cold of inland Norfolk. The light was bright, and the sun was high in the sky, glinting on the remnants of frost on the hard earth.

Long before they entered Norwich, they could see the great white royal castle perched above the surrounding land, its white stone from France overpowering the landscape, as it was meant to do. The only royal castle in Norfolk and Suffolk, it was a symbol of imperial power and dominance. Alice shivered and tried to look away, but she was still aware of it, casting its pervasive gaze across the city. The message was clear—the King was watching his subjects closely. Alice hoped he wasn't focused on them now. Stupid, she knew, as he was miles from here, drumming up support for his French campaign. But still, she felt a crawling down her spine.

The other symbol of dominance was the cathedral, a vast stone edifice asserting its equal rights to the hearts, minds, and souls of its inhabitants as the King. But to Alice, the cathedral was a thing of beauty, piercing the pale blue sky as if reaching to heaven. The castle was a thing of dominance, with no aspiration to heaven, only to earthly subjugation.

They passed through St. Augustine's Gate and were immediately plunged into the busyness that was Norwich. With over sixty parish churches and 15,000 people living in the confines of the city wall, the place was a hive of industry. The warehouses and wharves spoke of the flourishing trade, as did the elegant stone-built houses, newly built and so different to the wooden buildings found elsewhere in the city and country. And, of course, it was one of these impressive stone houses which was Savari's townhouse, set apart from the market, west, on a rise, flanked by other smart dwellings.

William let out a low whistle as they pulled up outside. He helped Alice off the horse and looked up at the building. "I knew he was doing well at court, but not this well."

Warin led the horses to the stables at the rear of the property, through a courtyard. A servant bid them enter.

They walked directly into the vaulted Hall. The smell of the newly sawn wood in the rafters combined with the earthiness of the decorated clay tiles. A bright fire was lit in a grate, above which a chimney took the smoke out of the room.

The door burst open, and Savari entered. He was the same height as William but not as broad. His face was extremely handsome, sculpted and intelligent and, thought Alice, slightly scary. Unlike William, you couldn't be sure what Savari was thinking.

He strode across the room and embraced William. "Brother!" He stepped back. "I had not expected to see you here this night." He turned his perceptive gaze to Alice. "Nor in such beautiful company."

"And I had not expected it either. There is a story to tell."

Savari took his eyes from Alice, and she breathed again. She felt as if she'd been examined, and a conclusion had been drawn. But she had no idea what that might be.

"Then come." He slapped William on the back once more. "Take a seat, and tell your story." He gave orders to the maid, who promptly disappeared. He turned a charming smile to Alice. If he were not William's brother, Alice wouldn't have trusted it. "And Lady Alice, perhaps you'd care to bathe before dinner?" He gestured to the stairs. "I made sure the house had all the newest features. There is a bath, and I've instructed my maid to go to a lady I know where she can gather some fresh clothes for you."

Alice was grateful for the courtesies. "Thank you, sir. And I will gladly avail myself of these luxuries, but before I do, I wish to be present for your talk with William."

Savari looked at William and raised an eyebrow. William shrugged. "It is her right. She is involved. We are both implicated in something which I'm hoping won't be bigger than either of us."

Savari's mouth clenched into a grim line. He indicated that their cups be replenished and then sat back, not partaking of any of the food which was set before them. "Then, please, tell me everything."

"Where to start?" murmured William.

"The salient point," said Savari.

William looked up from the depths of his cup and into Savari's eyes. "I killed a man."

Savari nodded as if this occurrence happened every day. "And who is this man?"

"Ralph de Gant."

Savari gave a tight gasp. He walked to a side table and picked up the wine. He paused and then uncorked it and poured wine into his empty cup. Then he turned. "Ah, William, that is indeed a salient point." He paused. "Another one would be, who witnessed it?"

"Alice," said William. "Warin, my squire, and Ralph's son, Adam."

Savari winced slightly at the last name. "And what kind of man is Adam?"

"He is still but a boy." William rolled his lips together and exchanged looks with Alice.

Alice turned to Savari. "A boy who should not be overlooked, I fear."

Savari shrugged. "We can deal with him. He is of no consequence or power at court. And Ralph's star was waning anyway. He'd become a thorn in the King's side. I don't think our King will miss him. In fact, he could be grateful for him being gone." He took another sip of wine. "I'll put the word out that the bandits in Lincolnshire have become bold, and are now attacking the Barons. Ralph made some unpopular decisions, which I'm sure can be made to be the reason for the murder. And, as to the boy, Adam, I'll track him down and persuade him to keep his peace."

William shook his head. "None of this was meant to happen."

"I'm sure," said Savari, looking from William to Alice and then back to William. "You were ever the gallant knight, plunging in where you shouldn't in the name of honor and truth."

"Aren't we all?" said William.

Savari grunted, and Alice got the feeling that Savari didn't agree with William. She felt a surge of love for William. His words were typical of him. He believed in the best of everyone. Unlike his brother, Alice thought, who she suspected believed the worst of everyone, as she did.

She turned suddenly to see Savari's eyes upon her. He'd been watching her watch William. She blushed as she remembered how her thoughts had been straying. Savari smiled, and for the first time, she saw some warmth in that smile. Maybe he sensed her feelings for William.

"And you, Lady Alice, what do you intend to do now?"

It was the first time anyone had asked her. Even William, for all his consideration, hadn't asked her what she wanted. He'd thought he'd known.

"I cannot return to my home, to the de Courcy castle. I fear I would be too vulnerable there. My father's cousin, Sir Bayard of Wrotham, has been promised a position at court. I heard them speak of the newly vacant Sheriff of Norfolk and Suffolk. His power is only increasing. He could return for me and try to marry me off to someone else. I cannot return there."

"Of course not," said William. "You will come to Wanham."

She shook her head. "I've sent word to the Abbess. She'll take me in, I'm sure."

A frown settled over William's brow, but he didn't argue, for which she was thankful. She knew he'd raise the subject later when they were alone.

Savari nodded and looked thoughtfully between his

brother and Alice. "And I'll do what I can at court to keep you all safe," said Savari.

"When do you return to court?" asked William, obviously wanting to change the subject from Alice's future.

"Tomorrow," replied Savari. "My business here is done." He looked at Alice. "I will do my best to protect your gallant knight, Lady Alice."

She drew a deep breath and gave him a quick, assenting smile. "Thank you." She rose. "I think I'll take that bath you mentioned now."

William and Savari both rose and bade her goodnight.

She followed the maid to her chamber, where a steaming bath had been prepared as Savari had promised. She peeled off her clothes and sank into its depths, and marveled at the luxury in which Savari lived.

Once clean, she allowed herself to lie back and succumb to the relaxation of the water and let her mind drift. This time not to the dark times but to William. He was like an oak tree, the one firm thing in this troubled land, and one to which she longed to cling. She sighed and imagined herself clinging to him.

There was a knock at the door, and she rose out the water and wrapped herself in the drying sheet. She padded across the wooden floor upon which a Turkish rug had been laid in a heathen style. Moonlight lay in strips across the floor. The wool was warm to her feet.

"Alice? It is William."

"One moment."

She pulled on her chemise, and flung a cloak around herself for modesty's sake, and opened the door. William stood outside, a candle sputtering in his hand, casting flickering shadows over his face. She nearly started back, as he didn't look like him. Again the memory of how he'd killed

Ralph cast her mind back to the fear that had gripped her when Bayard had visited her at nights.

He frowned and began to reach out to her but stopped and dropped his hand by his side. "There it is again, Alice. You almost look scared of me. I may be the one person in the world you should not be scared of. I would do anything for you, you must know that."

She nodded as he brought the light around and placed it on a ledge, and his features settled into their usual form once more. She released a tightly held breath. "I do know that."

"Then, unless you hear back from the Abbess, tomorrow we ride to Wanham, and we make preparations." He nodded and retreated as if there were nothing more to be said. By the time she'd drawn breath, he'd gone. She closed the door behind her.

Preparations, William had said. He meant plans. Plans to work out what would happen next. That's what he meant. Plans for her future. He could not have meant preparations, for that would assume a plan has been established. And they'd discussed nothing.

Alice climbed into bed and lay looking up at the ceiling, its newly hewn wood still redolent of the forest. She gripped the fur coverlet in the palms of her hands and drew in a long, deep breath. She swallowed. Tomorrow. She'd tell him tomorrow after they'd reached Wanham. Tomorrow, she insisted to herself, forcing her eyes to close and her breathing to slow. Tomorrow, she repeated, as her eyes opened wide once more.

CHAPTER 6

Despite her concerns, Alice had slept soundly and awoke refreshed and full of hope. She'd manage to find a way to make William understand, and she'd find a home with Lady Anne at the Priory. While it might not be the home that she'd dreamed of as a girl, it would be a home where she could work and be useful. It would be a good life.

A good life, she repeated to herself as she descended the stairs into Savari's Hall, where both men were already drinking their morning ale.

Savari's whistled in appreciation while William smiled warmly. Savari swept a low bow. "You are like an angel descending from the skies, my lady."

William turned away, but not before Alice noticed a scowl.

"And you, Savari," said William, pouring Alice a drink, "are like a court-fed popinjay. A flatterer."

"And where is your courtesy, brother?" asked Savari, not in the least offended.

"Lacking entirely," said William, shooting Alice a quick grin. "Alice knows what I think, and that is enough for me."

"But not enough for me," said Savari with a wicked grin. "Pray tell, Lady Alice, do you know my brother William's thoughts?"

"And how could I do that, sir?" She smiled, unable to resist Savari's charm. "When he speaks so little?"

William's eyes narrowed, but he said nothing and took a swig of ale instead.

"Ah, then I am correct," said Savari. "You quiet men are all alike. Simply because you think something, you believe it to be understood. You must tell the lady Alice exactly how you perceive her, or else she might believe you to be indifferent."

"Is that so, Alice?" asked William.

Alice's smile faltered, but with an encouraging nod from Savari, she shrugged. William must have taken the shrug, not for the denial she implied, but for uncertainty.

"Well then," he said. "You are the most beautiful woman I know or have ever known. I've never seen an angel, and I've no need to, for I've seen you."

Savari raised an eyebrow, and he clapped William on the back. "You, brother, have no need of courtly advice. You know more than any of us." He turned to Alice. "He's all yours."

Savari summoned his squire and disappeared to his office, leaving William and Alice in awkward silence.

Alice suddenly felt ashamed for joining Savari in teasing William, because she'd forced him to speak to her in a way she'd been trying to avoid.

"William, I'm sorry, I shouldn't have teased you so. I—"

"It's of no consequence."

"But it is, William. I'm sorry for making you speak out thus. It was wrong considering…" The words proved reluctant to emerge. She hadn't intended to have this conversation so soon.

He sat forward in his chair. "Considering what, Alice? Tell me."

She licked her lips. "Considering I sent word last night to Lady Anne at the Priory asking her permission to stay with her for the foreseeable future."

William's facial expression didn't change, only his eyes, in which she could see hurt, and something more, something akin to pain. It was quickly covered.

"And your mind is made up?"

She nodded.

"Hm," he grunted. "Mayhap Savari was right, I should have told you earlier how I feel about you. Mayhap then you'd reconsider this mad idea to live at the Priory."

She shook her head. "I cannot. At the Priory, I will have the life which I desire."

"And you desire no other?" His eyes were hot as they sought hers.

Alice was saved from answering by the return of Savari. "The horses are being readied for your journey. But come and breakfast first."

They'd hardly begun to break their fast when a messenger was shown into the room.

"My lady." The messenger bowed. "Word from Lady Anne, the Abbess. She says you must not come to the Priory for there is sickness there."

Alice leaped up. "Sickness? What kind? How many ail?"

The messenger shrugged. "I know not, my lady. All I know is the message that the Abbess gave me to give you. She said, there is illness, and she asks you not to come."

"And you know nothing of it?" asked Alice, confused by the messenger's lack of knowledge.

Another shrug.

William turned to Savari. "Is there sickness in the county?"

“Not that I’ve heard.” Savari turned to the messenger. “What kind of sickness?” They all knew what he meant.

“There is no plague. Only…”—the messenger shrugged —“some sickness. That is all I know,” said the messenger. “She specifically said the Lady Alice shouldn’t come.”

Alice’s heart sank. Her one hope of refuge from the vagaries of life had been dashed. It seemed she had no option but to continue to confront her fears.

ALICE RODE a palfrey borrowed from Savari for the last part of the journey to Wanham. William missed her body pressed against his. It had been the closest they’d been for years. He missed it, missed her. Like he was missing a part of himself. And he had a horrible feeling, in the pit of his gut, that that sense of loss wouldn’t be filled anytime soon.

As Wanham Castle came into view, he watched as people emerged and shouts rose over the flat lands. He was happy to be back, but it wasn’t the homecoming he’d imagined.

Even though he forced his eyes not to linger on Alice, he was aware of the tension in her shoulders, in the way she held the reins, and those beautiful lips of hers, pulled thinner than usual, no doubt from the same train of thought which puckered her brow. But, more than anything, the shadow which lay behind her eyes when she cast her gaze upon him chilled him, made him uncertain. And one of the things he hated most in this world was uncertainty.

“You’re thinking of your friends at the Abbey?” he asked.

“Aye. I’m concerned. I would rather be of help to them.”

“But it sounds as if the Abbess would rather you didn’t risk your health.”

She sighed, and it was the sound of hope leaving her soul. His already chilled heart pinched with pain. “I know,” she said. “I must be patient.”

"You don't wish to live at Wanham then." His voice was flat to his ears.

"I love Wanham and your sisters, you know that. It's just..."

"Just *me,* you don't like?" He didn't know from where such insecurity came. It wasn't something he could ever remember feeling for anyone else, only Alice.

"No!" she said quickly. "No," she repeated, as if wrenching the word from somewhere deep inside.

"Good. Then if neither my sisters nor I are the things that prevent you from living at Wanham, everything else can be overcome."

There was a shout and a wave as Lora ran toward them from the gatehouse, her dogs bounding either side of her.

"Will! Alice!" she panted. "Thank the Lord, you are both safe! We've been out of our minds with worry!"

With Lora's chatter filling the gaping silence which lay between him and Alice now, they entered the castle, his gaze drawn to her troubled one, unable to shake off the sense that Alice was keeping something from him. And he didn't have the first idea what it was. And wouldn't, until she was ready to tell him, which wouldn't be soon, given the way his sisters were crowding around her.

"Lora! Celestria! Give Alice room to breathe!" said Katherine, in her usual low voice which, despite its lack of force, was firm and obeyed by everyone except Celestria, whose passionate nature was hard to restrain.

"We thought you'd died!" cried Celestria.

Katherine shook her head in disbelief at her sister's dramatic delivery and embraced William.

Lora rolled her eyes as she held the two gray lurcher dogs so that they didn't add their enthusiasm to the welcome. "No, we didn't. We knew that if William was coming for you, Alice, you'd be safe."

Alice and William exchanged quick smiles. “And I am, thanks to him.”

“And you’ve come to stay here, that’s very good. Very good, indeed,” said Katherine. “We can keep you safe here, can’t we, brother?” she said with a smile.

He met Alice’s gaze. “I’ll make sure of it.”

But she looked away too quickly, and Katherine noticed and raised an eyebrow at William. He shrugged.

Celestria slipped her hand through Alice’s arm, and William, Katherine and Lora followed them into the Hall. It was dark inside, the light barely gaining entry in these shorter daylight hours of autumn. But William quelled his usual impatience to be outside.

Celestria brought Alice to the fire where she sat on one side with Katherine on the other. Lora stood with William, petting the dogs, while updating William on the estate. As much as he was interested in Lora’s news—she, alone of the girls, was most similar to him in his love of the outdoors—he was distracted by the conversation Celestria was having with Alice.

“Now, you must tell us everything that happened.” Celestria tucked her legs beneath her beautiful skirt, re-arranged them a little, and then looked expectantly at Alice.

“That, dear Celestria,” said Alice, accepting the warming cup of wine, “would take too long.”

Celestria pouted. “Only the highlights then.”

“Highlights,” said Alice, before twisting her lips into a grimace. “The only highlight was that I escaped from the castle with William.”

“But what happened?” insisted Celestria. “How did you escape?”

“Celestria!” admonished Katherine and William at the same time.

“What?” asked Celestria. “I only want to know whether or

not Sir Ralph will be knocking on our door any day soon. Whether there's danger lurking or not." She shrugged. "That's all."

William looked from one to the other. There was nothing for it but to tell the truth. "There's nothing to fear on that score. Ralph de Gant is dead."

William felt all eyes upon him. Even the dogs turned to him, as if absorbing the feelings of those around him.

"How?" Katherine's voice was cracked with emotion as if dreading what she'd hear. She licked her lips and repeated the word, stronger this time. "How?"

"I killed him. I had no choice."

Katherine bit her lip and looked away. "So much bloodshed. When will it end?"

"When people stop coveting what is ours," he said grimly.

"And Alice *is* ours, is she not?" asked Celestria. She didn't wait for a reply. "So, you are to marry my brother." Celestria sat back with a self-satisfied smile. "I told Katherine you would, but she wouldn't listen to me."

"Celestria! A man has been killed. And all you can think of is marriage?" asked Katherine.

Celestria shrugged. "Life goes on." She glanced at Lora. "At least Lora won't have to marry a de Gant now. Her betrothal to Sir Ralph's son must be well and truly null and void after all that's happened."

William had completely forgotten that the lad who'd witnessed the murder had been affianced to Lora. It had been something of his father's doing many years before if he remembered aright, but which had lapsed over the years since his father's death.

He exchanged a grim look with Alice. "Adam de Gant will not be seeking marriage to Lora, that much I can tell you."

"Thank the Lord for that," said Lora, apparently unperturbed. "I have no wish to marry."

Celestria rolled her eyes. "You will. Everyone does. Exactly as William and Alice are about to."

"Are you getting married, Will?" asked Lora.

There was an awkward silence. He shook his head.

"No, Lora," said Alice, and William's heart sank even further.

"But, you *will* be staying here, won't you?" asked Katherine.

"Until the sickness at the abbey has passed and then I'll go to the Priory to live."

"Oh," the girls exclaimed in confused unison.

"But why?" Celestria looked grief-stricken.

"Because…" began Alice.

William waited to hear Alice's reply. He was as interested as his sisters.

"Because"—Alice's gaze steadied, and she focused on him —"I think it would be for the best."

Katherine bit her lip and looked away.

William had seen enough. Alice couldn't wait to leave Wanham *and* him. Her disappointment at not being able to go directly to the Abbey was written plainly across her face. *His* Alice didn't want him, or anything he could offer—except protection. And she hadn't even asked for that.

~

THE DAYS GREW shorter as the weeks passed into months and as Christmas fast approached, life fell into a pattern, far easier and more joyful than Alice could remember ever experiencing. They were days during which she'd managed to avoid being alone with William, days in which she gradually came to the conclusion that the Abbess didn't want her at the Priory. The sickness had been confined to only two people, both of whom had since recovered. But still, the Abbess was too busy to see her.

And now, as she paused in the courtyard, her attention snagged by the sight of William, she wondered if her old resolve was as firm as it had been. He was stripped to the waist, despite the chill, as he brought down the hammer on the horseshoe which he held in tongs over a blazing furnace. His body glistened in the firelight as he exerted himself with steady focus. The crash of metal upon metal vibrated through her body until she could almost feel his touch upon her, inside her.

She shivered, and one of the dogs beside her barked, and William looked over and caught her gaze. He turned, gave one sharp blow of the hammer, and tossed the horseshoe into a bucket of cold water where it hissed, and sent up a cloud of steam. He said something to the person helping him and walked over to her.

She should go. She should make her legs move. She should walk away. But instead, her eyes lowered to his chest, following a trickle of sweat as it coursed down his soot-streaked skin. She swallowed.

"Alice," he greeted, coming to a halt close to her so that she had no choice but to gaze at that muscled chest. "Where are you going?"

"To gather some holly for the Hall."

"Then I will come with you." He pulled on his shirt as he fell into step with her. She fixed her eyes on the rough trodden path, which led to a walled garden.

She'd left it late. The sun had barely shown its face during the day and, all too soon, had begun its drop back into night. The air was damp, as well as cool now, and held a misty atmosphere of something Alice would have described as like expectation, if it weren't impossible.

William reached in front of her, and she was startled by

his proximity as he pulled open the door to the walled garden.

"Thank you," she said, feeling almost shy. She should make some excuse. *She should.* She'd been avoiding being alone with him for weeks, but the words didn't form, and she knew, deep down, why not—because she wanted to be alone with him, despite all that she feared from him.

"You're welcome," he said, as he followed her into the deserted garden, past a spider's web. The web gleamed in the low, misty light, droplets of mist clinging to the strands as the dark body of the spider scurried into a corner, patiently awaiting its dinner.

She breathed deeply of the smell of the remnants of autumn, the last of the fruit still clinging with stolid desperation to its branches, which were trained to grow along the warmth of the old wall. The winter white blooms seemed to glow in the unearthly light.

"I've always loved this place," said Alice dreamily, brushing the soft petals of a rose with her fingers as she passed. She bobbed down and picked a rose from the path which must have fallen from someone's basket. When she stood up, William held out her basket, and she dropped it in.

"That's because it suits you. You belong here."

Alice suddenly felt uncomfortable and stepped back onto the path. "No, I do not think it is that."

"I do. You belong in such beauty, just as I belong outside, in the fields and lands beyond these walls." He picked the rose from the basket. "You're like this rose. Delicate and full of beauty." He lifted it to his nose. "Both inside and out."

She reached out and laid her hand on the rose, and he looked into her eyes. "William, I am but a regular woman. You think me delicate and beautiful, and, while that is flattering—"

"I do not say such things to flatter. I say them for they are true."

She smiled. "While that is flattering," she repeated firmly. "It is true I am like this rose. Not because it is delicate, on the contrary, it has already survived frosts long after other more apparently robust blooms have fallen. And also"—she twisted the rose around in his hands—"it is bruised. Like me. Faulty."

A shadow crossed his eyes as if what she'd said had truly hurt him. He shook his head and licked his lips. "No, Alice. Don't say such things. There is no fault in you."

She placed her hand gently on his. "But there is. More than you know." She pulled her hand away when his hand closed over hers. "Like tarrying when I should be working."

She stepped in front of him and slipped out the rear gate where the air was chill and damp, and the garden more wild. It was where the holly trees grew, shrouding the fish pond with dark shadows, dwarfed by the gnarly oaks which lined the lane behind them. The holly trees were darkly green, and red berries dotted their depth. "These will do nicely."

William narrowed his eyes and half-smiled. "Trying to talk with you, Alice de Courcy, is like trying to catch the sunlight." He paused. "Not only impossible, but in the end you realize simply being in the sunlight is enough."

Alice laughed and felt warm inside. For all her resistance, she'd found a comfort in William's company over the past weeks, providing he wasn't alone. She'd come to look for him first in a room, and to talk with him, and to wonder what he was doing. It was only now that she realized that something had changed within her. Not her intentions, no, they were the same. Still, they were more difficult to adhere to, because somehow William had caught the cords which bound her to him, and had tightened them, drawing her closer into his orbit.

They spent the last hour of daylight in light-hearted

banter, with Alice directing William—who appeared to need some coaxing, usually in the form of her taking hold of his arm and directing him—to cut down the large branches needed to decorate the Hall. She watched, unable to prevent herself from laughing as he pretended to find things harder than they were, as she cut the sprigs for the yule log and table decorations.

With their arms full, they retraced their steps back into the walled garden, with William dragging the spiky branches along the mossy path. Inside there was less light than outside, which still captured the last shreds of misty daylight.

He stopped her before they left the walled garden. His hand was on her arm, but he exerted no pressure.

"Know this, Lady Alice de Courcy," he said in an undertone that she felt in every part of her. "I will discover what it is you're afraid of, and I will take that fear away from you if it's the last thing I do."

She narrowed her eyes and averted her gaze. She didn't want him to see that most likely it *would* be the last thing he'd do. Because he'd never find out.

She was secure in the knowledge that he wouldn't find out. Because how could she tell him that it was him she was afraid of?

CHAPTER 7

The Hall was full of people and heavy with the scent of beeswax and baking, and the fresh green boughs of holly, bay, and yew still with the chill of winter upon them. While Katherine supervised the kitchen, Celestria flirted with the mummers and musicians, and Alice managed the decorating of the Hall.

It was the first time she'd ever had any say in how to decorate the Hall for Christmas. Her mother had always exerted total control of every aspect of her life until now. Alice hadn't heard from her mother since she'd left to live with her brother in the Border country. She'd received word that she'd arrived there safely, but nothing since. She hoped she was living a better life than she had in Norfolk.

But, as she stepped away from the central display of greenery to appraise it, the sense of apprehension which continued to linger at the edges of her mind made her doubt it.

"I think it should go a little more to the right," she said, firmly pushing her fears to the back of her mind.

Lora rolled her eyes. "It's in the center already!"

Alice shook her head. "Not quite."

"Come down, Lora," said William. "And we'll move it along as Alice says."

Alice smiled at William. It seemed she could do no wrong in his eyes, despite her unwillingness to commit to him.

Lora jumped down from the table, and William adjusted the rope which had been looped over the central beam. It was at the end of this that they were fixing the twelve bundles of greenery—a combination of holly, mistletoe, and whatever scented herbs Alice could find—which would comprise the kissing bush.

The rope was duly moved over a little, and the process began again.

William came and stood beside Alice. "You know, I think Lora was right. It *was* near enough." But he said it with a smile.

"Everything has to be right, William. I can't bear it when it's not."

William frowned a little and turned to face her, bringing his head closer to her as if to speak confidentially. "You know, sometimes near enough is good enough. Things don't have to be perfect."

She knew he wasn't referring to the decorations, but to her. She brushed some stray yew leaves from her gown.

"It's best that everything is in its rightful place," she said firmly. Only then did she believe she could conceal her inner flaws—the things which were too humiliating for her to show.

"Why is that so important to you, Alice?"

"Because…" She trailed off as she tried to think of how she could explain such a deep-rooted feeling within her, without giving away too much. She shrugged. "Because anything could happen if it's not."

William's perceptive glance made her realize she hadn't

succeeded. She lowered her gaze, but he reached out and turned her face to his with a light touch of his finger upon her cheek.

"Anything? Like what?"

She sucked in a breath as she tried to frame the words which surfaced in her mind, things she dreaded because there was only one thing which lay at the end of that road of chaos, and that was pain. She'd felt its blow before and couldn't bear, not only to feel it again but to allow others to know of it. She knew that their love was based upon how they saw her now, not how she truly was.

She shook her head. "I'm being fanciful." She gave a quick smile and glanced over his shoulder, desperate to avoid meeting his eyes. "Just like Celestria."

But he didn't shift his gaze. "Stop it, Alice. You must. I know what you're doing. You're avoiding telling me of what it is that so scares you. It runs deep, that much I know."

"Nay, William. What could I be frightened of now?"

"That I know not, but I can see you are afeared of something. And I will find out, Alice, I will."

Suddenly a shout of laughter made them both turn around. With everyone focused on their own work, Celestria's flirting had ended up with her sitting on a mummer's lap.

"Celestria!" growled William. "Come here!"

She jumped up and gave her gown a twirl for the benefit of the mummers. "What is it, brother?"

"Behave yourself!"

"I'm only having fun. If you'd let me go to court with Savari, I wouldn't be so bored."

"Savari says it's no place for a girl like you. Or any girl, come to that."

"Any girl who wants to have fun!"

Celestria flounced away to play with the dogs, her every

move designed to appeal to the mummers' eyes—especially one.

"I don't like the way that mummer is looking at Celestria," said William, narrowing his gaze.

Alice followed his glance. "I fear it is the way most men look at her. She is beautiful and lively and I think her desire for men is strong." She looked at William, hoping that she hadn't gone too far. But it was something of which she was particularly aware because it was something she felt to be entirely lacking in herself.

"I fear you're right. We need to get her married as soon as possible, otherwise there will be trouble."

Alice couldn't help thinking there would be trouble whatever happened but didn't want to worry William any more than he already was. She shrugged. "She wants to live life. She's too big for this world, here at Wanham."

William turned his penetrating gaze to Alice. "Is that what you think, too?"

She shook her head and picked up a piece of holly, trimming it to fit over the doorways. She handed it to a servant to hang. "No, of course not. If anything, Wanham is too big for me. I'd be better somewhere quieter."

He grunted. "You're wrong, you know."

She blinked, surprised. William rarely contradicted her. She wasn't sure she liked it. "I don't believe so."

He grunted again, but this time didn't do anything except give her a sideways glance.

She plucked another piece of greenery, with an exaggerated flick of the wrist. "And what does that mean?"

"What?"

"That look. That grunt."

"Just that you always think you're right, and you're not. Sometimes, other people are right."

"Like you, I suppose."

"Yes, like me. And you should give their views—*my* views—due consideration. To do otherwise"—he hesitated but plowed on—"shows arrogance."

Alice dropped the bough with which she'd been fiddling. "I'm arrogant now, am I?"

"Aye, you are." And with that, he strode away.

Alice didn't know what surprised her more—his accusation of arrogance, or his abrupt departure. She was accustomed to William's devotion, even if she believed it to be unwarranted. They'd had a quarrel; they never quarreled.

She was about to follow him, to say what, she had no idea, when Katherine caught her attention. Her face was flushed with the heat from the kitchen, but it wasn't that which was so arresting. Alice had never seen Katherine look so agitated.

"What is it, Katherine? What's happened?"

Katherine pulled a face. "Problems with our goods at Yarmouth. I've been trying to track down the captain of the boat, but I can't find him. He only ever seems to appear when I don't want him and not be there when I do!"

"That sounds strange." And, indeed, Alice did think that Katherine's reaction was quite unlike her normal sensible one. She seemed oddly rattled by this mysterious sea captain, who always appeared to be so provoking to her.

"Strange isn't the word for it."

Alice wondered what word it should be, but decided not to ask. Katherine appeared to be unusually preoccupied.

"It's looking good," said Lora as she swept into the Hall on a wave of cold air.

Alice followed her gaze as she looked around the Hall, which had been transformed—every inch filled with greenery brought in from all around the estates. Evergreen branches—not only holly, but laurel and yew—decorated the walls, the windows and were draped around and on the tables. And above them, the ceiling was festooned with an outrageous display of greenery.

Lora laughed. "No need for me to be outside with this lot! It's like being in a green cave!" She pointed to the bright red ribbons which secured small branches grouped into twelves. "I see you managed to get Celestria to yield her ribbons for the decorations."

"Aye. It took some doing," said Alice. Truth was, she'd grown closer to Celestria over the past weeks than she'd imagined. Celestria was so headstrong she took no notice of Alice's withdrawn temperament, nor the barriers Alice tried to place between her and everyone else. Celestria simply bowled right on through them. It made things easier in some ways. And it made Alice wish that she could be like that with the others, especially William.

Lora breathed in deeply. "Um, it smells good too. I'm starving."

"You'll have to wait until our guests arrive," said Katherine, whose agitation had increased, if anything.

It turned out that they didn't have to wait long. Soon the Hall was full, not only with their friends and neighbors, but the poor folk who lived thereabouts. They were all brought forth on that chill winter evening with the promise of good food and wine and company—exactly as their forefathers had done on the eve of Christ's birth for centuries before them.

A shout of "Wassail!" silenced the guests as they found their seats. Then Sir Harry, as Surveyor for the evening, turned to William, as the most honored guest and asked if the feast could begin.

"No!" said William. "Not until First Foot cross the Christmas threshold!"

Suddenly from the rear of the Hall, the mummer with the darkest hair appeared, dressed from head to toe in green. He was carrying an evergreen bough and wore small bells on bands around his ankles. Half-dancing, half-skipping, he moved toward the high table and, with a flourish, jumped over the green line of cloth which marked the Christmas threshold. Miraculously he found himself close to Celestria, who burst into peals of laughter. William shot the mummer a black look.

Once Christmas had been 'let in', and Christmas joy invited inside, the candles and yule log were lit and, to cheers of "Wassail! Wassail!", everyone fell to the feast of frumenty, roast meats, fish and fowl, and sweet morsels of gingerbread figures, plum puddings, and mince pies. It was all washed down with copious amounts of wine—sweet pear, elderberry, and the finest from Gascony.

This must be what having a family is like, thought Alice, as she watched Savari talking with William, and the girls dance along with everyone else. The thump of feet as they landed on the wooden floor in time to the drum, mingled with the pipes and shouts and laughter. The Hall was warm from the fires, full of the scent of pine and beeswax.

"Are you sure you don't wish to dance?" asked William, as Savari took to the floor with Lora.

She shook her head. "No. But you must."

"If you don't wish to, then neither do I."

There was something comforting about that, despite her protestations.

"Who is that man Celestria is trying to flirt with?" asked William.

Alice followed William's gaze. "Oh, that's that sea captain who Katherine is having so much trouble with."

"He looks pretty much at home here. What's he doing here, anyway?"

"Katherine seems as surprised as anyone that he turned up."

"I wonder what he wants?"

"Not Celestria by the looks of things," said Alice, noting how Celestria's advances were going unmet. Instead, the captain's dark gaze swept across the room and settled on Katherine, who continued to dance. Alice suddenly realized what kept Katherine dancing. She was avoiding this man.

Celestria sat beside them with a flounce. "That man is horrible. Why, do you know he was rude to me? He told me to go and amuse myself elsewhere with young boys. He dismissed me as if I were nothing but a nuisance child!"

Alice tried not to smile.

William glanced in the sea captain's direction. "That man has gone up in my estimation."

Celestria grunted with annoyance and broke off a piece of marchpane, and sat back and munched on it.

"There are plenty of others with whom you can dance," said Alice.

"I don't *want* to dance with anyone else."

"There must be someone," said Alice, looking around. When she looked back at Celestria, her eyes had narrowed, and she knew that she'd found something else to entertain her.

"Yes, there is." Celestria swallowed the marchpane and jumped up. "I'll dance if you will." She took hold of Alice's hand and tried to pull her to the floor.

"No! I don't dance. I don't wish to dance."

"Yes, you do. I know you want to, for I saw your foot tapping in time to the drum."

Indeed, Alice had loved to dance as a young girl before everything changed. But she never allowed herself to relax in company since that time. She shook her head.

Celestria gave a playful pout. "If you don't dance, I'll sit and sulk and make everyone's life a misery. You know I will, you know I can do it."

Alice sighed; she certainly did know. Celestria ignored the chill exterior Alice showed to the world—she didn't seem aware of it. And, so, when Celestria tugged at her hand again, she surrendered to the music and Celestria's will, and suddenly found herself in the midst of a mass of people, all jumping and moving to the music.

Her body soon remembered the long-forgotten rhythms and steps of the dances, and she twirled and jumped with the best of them. As the second dance drew to a close, she was swung around and found herself in William's arms.

Then the music stopped, and Alice was aware of nothing except William's arms, which stayed around her, and his head dipped to hers, smiling. Then suddenly he looked up, and Alice was aware of Celestria shouting something at them and pointing overhead. Alice looked up to find that she and William were standing beneath the kissing bush of mistletoe, decorated with ribbons, small oranges and apples, nuts and tiny sculptures molded from stiff cloth.

William lowered his head to hers. "We must kiss, Alice, it is tradition."

Alice nodded anxiously. She knew it was and had avoided it all evening. It was only the dancing which had made her unaware of her position in the Hall—immediately beneath the kissing bush.

Her breathing quickened as William dipped his head to hers, his eyes closing as he drew nearer. For a moment, she stiffened in his arms, but then she felt the gentling touch of his hand behind her head, and his lips brush hers. She gasped as the touch lit something inside of her and the spark spluttered into life and flickered, a reminder of what life should be like, before he pulled away and the light went out, leaving her colder than before, knowing the heat she'd been missing, heat with which she wanted to fill herself again.

She was surprised to find her arms were already placed

higher on his back than before the kiss, and she resisted his backward move. Instead, she lifted her face to his, and he smiled, a very male smile, and lowered his mouth to hers once more. And this time, she greeted his lips with her own. And there was no tentative brushing, but a growing fierceness which instantly ignited that flame once more. Except this time it didn't fade. It grew in strength, consuming the cold and dark, and sending tingles of desire along her skin and deeper, shooting inside of her, stirring her like echoes of long ago.

All her nerves were forgotten—everything was swept away under the intensity of his mouth upon hers. She felt him groan against her lips as she opened her mouth against his, wanting more. Then suddenly, she was aware of a change around her. It slowly filtered through her senses, and as William pulled away, she realized what it was. There was silence. She twisted around to find everyone was looking at them—some with open-mouthed astonishment, others with big grins. It was Celestria who broke the spell.

'Come, musicians!' she called out. 'Why have you stopped playing? Have you never seen a couple in love before?'

Everyone laughed, and the dancing began. But Alice was horrified. She felt humiliated and let down, not by anyone else, but by herself. She looked back at William, who appeared indifferent to his sister's words or the attention of the others. He was looking at her with a frown. He shook his head and held firmly onto her hand.

"Alice! Ignore Celestria. Ignore them all. It was only a kiss."

"Only a kiss?" she whispered. She doubted he would have heard over the din of the music and whoops and shouts of the dancers as they spun around them. "Only a kiss?" she repeated, more loudly. She felt naked, exposed to the world, and he thought it was only a kiss?

"To them, it was only a kiss. But for me?" He shook his head.

Rather than making her feel better, it made her feel worse —trapped by the intensity he conveyed through his hand. She shook her head and pulled her hand away as if it were being burned.

"I can't…" She looked around for an escape. "I'm sorry, but I can't do this, William." She hurried outside to the cold courtyard, lit by bright braziers. Rain had begun to fall, and she welcomed its dousing effect on her heated skin. She sucked in a deep chill breath, wanting to snuff out the fire which had been lit inside her by the kiss. But she feared it wasn't working, for her heart still quickened, and her lips tingled, reminding her of the kiss which had begun something she had no intention of finishing.

The sound of a door closing behind her made her turn around. William walked over to her. But he didn't keep his distance as he had before. Instead, he gripped her hands and talked to her fiercely.

"You cannot deny it, Alice—what passed between us in there. You cannot."

"And I do not. But I also cannot deny another truth."

His frown darkened. "And what is that?"

"That despite what…" She hesitated as she tried to frame words to describe what happened in the Hall. But she could not. "What happened in there, there can be nothing more."

"But we will marry," William said firmly. "I would not dream of anything other than marriage to you."

Tears sprung to her eyes at how honorable he was, and how it made no difference.

"Listen to me, William. I cannot marry you. I cannot live with you. I cannot give you the life you want."

"Why not?"

"Because I am not the person you think I am."

He hadn't expected that answer. He opened his mouth to speak but shook his head instead. William was always so sure of everything: his land, his family, and, he obviously believed, her. She'd turned his world upside down. And, while she regretted it deeply, he had to understand that marriage wasn't something she could inflict upon him. He thought he knew her, but he knew little of what had happened in the intervening years, when communication between their families had ceased. And she wanted it kept that way. William believed the best in people. She didn't want to be the one to open his eyes to the worst in people.

She backed away. "It has to be this way," she said more gently, her heart breaking. "I will not marry you, William."

"Until you tell me why, I will not believe you. We were meant to be together, Alice. You cannot deny that."

And she couldn't.

"I take your silence as agreement. Then what stands between us?"

Everything, she wanted to scream. Instead, she drew in a level breath. "I cannot give you what you want."

"All I want is you, and a family."

"And *that,* dear William, is what I cannot give you."

He looked stunned. "What do you mean?'

"I'm not the woman you think me to be."

"For the sake of the blessed virgin, would you please tell me what you are speaking of!"

She bit her lip and fixed her eyes on him, willing the courage to flow. "I am not like other women. The thought of lying with a man, even you, fills me with dread. I am not meant for marriage."

CHAPTER 8

William tried to stem the panic, to focus on the words which she'd wielded to such devastating effect. "What are you saying, Alice? I don't understand. What are you talking about?"

He wasn't aware of his hands tightening around her arms, only noticed it when she tried to pull away from him. He dropped his hands and stepped away as if he'd been forced, not by mere words, but by an iron fist, such was her sudden chill expression. He shook his head.

"Don't you do this, Alice," he said with a quiet rumble. But her cool look didn't leave her. "Don't hide from me. Don't you do this to me, or yourself, Alice!" His voice was louder now, but it still appeared to make no impact on her frozen features. He backed away. He could no more lay hands upon her than clutch at the sky. He clenched his fists instead, trying to contain the growing sense of frustration and panic which filled him as he sensed Alice moving away from him. "Alice!"

She gave a small, controlled shake of the head.

She'd gone inward, turned into that cool being that others

saw. Now, for the first time, he saw that woman—a stranger. His Alice, the real woman behind that beautiful exterior, was hidden from him. She'd done that. Retreated behind the curtain, which she used to keep open for him. It hurt him more than a knife to his body.

"I don't understand," he repeated.

"I've said the words, William. You must understand them." She calmly drew in a breath, quite unlike his own labored breathing. "I cannot have children."

"But why should you believe such a thing? How can you *know* such a thing?"

"Because..." She trailed off, and that chill exterior disappeared in an instant, and tears sprung to her eyes. She gave a cry like a caged animal and ran off across the courtyard and out through the gatehouse.

He glanced briefly at the open Hall from which music, heat and singing and stamping emerged. It seemed a different world, a lifetime since he and Alice had danced as carefree as any of the other partners in the Hall, and yet in a few moments everything had changed. He headed out the gatehouse to find her.

ALICE TOOK refuge where she always did, the church, next to Wanham Castle. From her first visit, she'd felt at peace there. Now, with the wind buffeting around her, echoing the confusion raging inside of herself, she ran through the rain as soon as she'd left the castle. By the time she collapsed against the gray studded doors of the church, she was wet to the bone.

She fumbled for the iron handle and twisted it. A gust of wind helped her open the heavy door, and she stumbled down the steps inside. On her knees, she looked up at the image of Jesus on the cross, stretched across the rood screen, and for the first time in an age, wept. She wept for all that she was losing, and wept for the sorrow she was causing the man she loved most in the world.

As she bowed her head in prayer, seeking guidance and strength, she heard the door open behind her and felt the fingers of the cold wind seeking out her damp clothes. She shivered and turned to see William standing looking at her.

"William!"

"Did you think I wouldn't come?" He shook his head. "Sometimes, Alice, I wonder if you even know me."

"I *know* you, William de Vere. And that is why I must walk away. I cannot ruin your life."

"You will do exactly that if you do not marry me."

"I will do that if I marry you. Have you not heard what I've said? I will never bear a child."

"Only God knows that for sure."

"No, I know it also."

"How?"

She swallowed. She'd never told anyone before. Only those persons involved knew what had happened all those years before, and they all had their reasons not to say anything. But now, looking into her dear William's eyes, she knew she could no longer keep it from him. That much she owed him.

"I'm not who you think I am," she said.

"I think you're Lady Alice de Vere. Are you not?" he asked with a smile.

"Aye, that is my name. But I'm not the girl you knew when we were young." She knew the moment he caught the thread of her meaning for a darkness entered his eyes.

"You..." He hesitated and licked his lips as he tried to find the words which were so abhorrent to him. What he didn't realize was that they were equally abhorrent to her. "You are not a maid?"

She shook her head. "I am not."

He angled his head and blinked. "You have lain with a man?"

She didn't move her eyes from his. She owed him that much. "I have." He closed his eyes, but not before she could see the pain there. "But you must know it was not willingly."

The replacement of pain with anger was swift. "Who was he?" His voice sent shivers along her already chilled body.

"I cannot say."

"You would protect this man?"

"Protect him? Nay, William. I would protect you, because I know you. And I know what you could do to such as he."

"Is that so bad? So wrong?"

"What is wrong is that you will be punished for such wrong-doing. And that, I could never bear. Promise me you won't."

But William appeared in no mind to make such a promise. "And why do you believe this rape," he said, spitting out the word, "will stop you from bearing a child?"

It had come to it. That point where there was no going back.

"Because I have made a promise before God that I will never lie with a man ever in my life again. I cannot. I *will* not."

His face was blank with shock. Silently, he pulled her to his body and held her close. The fine wool of his best surcote pressed against her cheek, giving her warmth and comfort, but that was all he could give. She had to be firm.

She pulled away. "You hold me now, and it is good. But I seek no more intimate touch. After what I went through, I cannot think of lying with a man again. It is not something I want."

He held her firmly at arms' length. "Listen to me, Alice de

Courcy. This is something that can be overcome if you still love me. Do you?"

She looked at him sadly. He was her beloved William, but he was also a man, with a man's pride, and a man's needs. He might think he could do without children, that she'd come around to welcoming him physically, but she knew what such rancor could do to people, she'd seen it first-hand with her parents. There was only one thing she could do for him now.

She shook her head. "I do not wish to marry you, William. The only relationship I desire is a spiritual one. I want to go to the Priory to live and work there as a healer."

"You cannot mean that."

"I *do* mean it. And you must accept that."

"I will *never* accept that."

She gripped his hands. "William. If you care for me, you must let me go. You must let me find my own way in life, for it cannot be with you. I have nothing to give you."

"I want nothing. Only you."

She had to be strong. She needed him to understand because she couldn't bear the thought of him growing to hate her for everything she couldn't give him. She sucked in a cold breath, trying to find the courage she needed.

"But *I* do not want you." There, it was said. And the moment she'd finished speaking she saw its effect on William, and she wished she could withdraw it. It hurt her like a physical ache to see such pain in his eyes. But it had to be done.

He stepped away as if pushed, walked to the door and opened it for her. She swept past him and retraced her steps back to the castle, with William following a few steps behind. She didn't stop until she was at the gatehouse when she could bear the silence no longer. She waited for him to catch up.

"I'll stay one more night, William. But then I must leave. It is past time."

She proceeded through to the Great Hall where the dancing continued, and their entrance went unnoticed. She went upstairs to the sisters' room where she packed her things, undressed, and lay staring at the ceiling. Below her, the festivities continued, without her and William. She'd leave first thing in the morning. She couldn't wait another day.

Eventually, the sisters retired for the night and lay beside her, but she feigned sleep. There was nothing to be gained by speaking to them. She'd talk to them in the morning if William hadn't. She thought Katherine would understand but she couldn't take the puzzled and hurt expressions from Lora or Celestria. They loved their brother unreservedly, and she doubted if they'd ever forgive her. Not at first anyway. But, in time, she hoped they'd come to understand.

She pulled the covers around her and closed her eyes, praying for sleep to come. It didn't.

THE NEXT DAY, William left early to ride to see Lady Anne at the Priory. A sleepless night had only been drawn to a close by his decision to see the Abbess.

When he entered the Priory, he was brought immediately to the Abbess. There was a roaring fire and comfortable and expensive decorations. It was the Hall of a wealthy and powerful woman.

"Lady Anne." He bowed respectfully.

"Sir William."

"I'm sorry to visit at such a time."

She graciously waved her arm. "I was expecting your visit. Although I must confess that I'd hoped it would come later."

"But—" William began, confounded by her admission.

"Please," she said, "take a seat." She nodded to a nun who disappeared, returning moments later with a tray of drinks. She waited until the drinks had been served before talking again. "No doubt you thought it strange when I forbade Alice to come here."

William shrugged. "There was illness…" He trailed off, because he had, indeed, thought it strange.

"Not so much as to prevent her from coming. I didn't want her here because I believed her future to be with you."

William was surprised and comforted to have the Abbess seemingly on his side. "Aye, I also believed she would marry me. But she insists she cannot."

"Because?" prompted the Abbess.

The words rolled around in his mouth, fighting to emerge. "Because," he repeated, "of what happened to her. Because of the gross violation she suffered."

"Ah," said the Abbess, sitting back. "And I take it you desire intimacy, desire children?"

"I wish I did not. But I cannot lie. I am a man, with a man's needs and desires. What I want to know is who was responsible."

"I will not say. What is important is that, if you truly love her, you must help her to heal, to come to terms with what happened to her, and then, mayhap, you will both lead a life of intimacy and happiness."

He shook his head. "I cannot marry her."

The Abbess looked up at William, stunned.

"You cannot?" she repeated.

"No. It is not what she wants."

"Maybe, at present, but it's what she needs."

He shook his head.

"Then why are you here, William? I'd assumed it was to consider how best to woo Alice?"

"Alice isn't a child to be wooed or not. She's a grown woman with a heart and mind of her own. And one which I respect. She says she doesn't want me, and I must abide by that."

"She said those very words?"

"Aye, she did."

The Abbess grunted. "Then she's more determined than I thought." The Abbess stared at him. "She must love you more than I believed."

William frowned. "She does not. That is the point, my lady. She will not have me because she does not love me enough."

"Ah, William. I believe you underestimate her."

He shook his head and rose. "I came here to make sure that you can take her. She's determined to come, and I cannot stand in her way any longer."

"She can come if she wishes. She would have made a better wife, but she'll make an excellent healer and nun, too."

William rose, grieved that his mission had been successful. "I will bring her to you this day."

He bowed and left the chamber, his heart heavier than when he'd first arrived.

As he approached Wanham Castle, he passed beneath a tree, and his horse whinnied and reared, as a lad dropped from the tree and stood in their tracks. By the time William controlled his horse, he realized it was no lad, but his sister, Lora.

"Lora! What were you doing up there?"

"Waiting for you!"

"You look like a hoyden. You have leaves in your hair, and your breeches are covered in mud. And I thought Katherine had forbidden you to wear breeches."

Lora shrugged and gave a cheeky smile, which always made people forget their anger. "I was playing with the dogs. Anyway, you took longer than I thought. Where did you go?"

"To the Abbey."

She groaned and swung a stick at some long grass. "So she's really going."

For all her tomboyish ways, Lora had an empathy for people and animals, which went beyond the usual. "It's what she wants."

"She doesn't really. Don't you see? She's worried about you. I think she's frightened of men. I've seen her as they approach her. She hides behind her deafness. I don't think she's as deaf as she appears."

William opened his eyes wide. He thought Lora had probably more insight into Alice's mind than Alice did. He shrugged. "I don't know. All I know is that she's determined to become a nun and live at the Priory. I've been to see the Abbess this morning, and she supports her decision."

"So, what are you going to do now?"

"I'm going back to the castle and I'll escort Alice to the Priory when she wishes to leave."

"She's all packed up," said Lora miserably.

"Then I will retrace my steps." He mounted his horse again. "Do you want a ride to the castle?"

She shook her head. "No. I can't bear to see her go."

"Nor can I, but we must. It is what she wants. And God knows she's had little enough of what she wants in her life."

He looked back to see Lora retreating into the marshes, like the wild girl she was. He turned forward again and rode hard to the castle.

Alice was waiting for him, her back to the fire, her bags, and cloak in readiness.

"William," she greeted him.

He forced himself to stand apart from her. But every inch

felt magnified as if she were far away already. "The Abbess has agreed."

The knife that was already in his heart twisted as he saw Alice's relief at his words. She nodded. "Good." She looked up at him, her cool demeanor restraining all that he knew would be going on inside of her. "Then it is time to leave."

With his heart breaking, William took the horse from the stable lad and walked it over to the block where Alice mounted her palfrey before he jumped onto his own. With only Warin for company, they set forth to the Priory, to the place which would swallow his Alice whole and never let her go again. Taking with her the only things that had ever had any meaning to his heart. But sometimes it seemed that to love someone meant that you had to embrace a broken heart, because you loved that person more than yourself.

They trotted slowly up the lane, neither of them looking left or right, only straight on. Only straight on because if he didn't, he thought he might release the roar of anguish, which was building inside of him. And he couldn't do that.

So with each silent mile, he pushed back the tide of emotion until it was stopped, deep inside where he would never see it, or experience it again. He'd make sure of that. Because to do otherwise was too painful. He could fight men to the death, he could weather any amount of discomfort or ills, but there was only one place he was vulnerable—his heart. But he knew that he'd have to fight this battle daily, to ensure his heart remained iron-clad.

CHAPTER 9

Alice had been at the Priory over a week, and a sense of peace was still eluding her.

It wasn't as if she was doing anything different. With the change in seasons, various sicknesses had sprung up as was usual, and Alice's healing skills were in demand.

That morning she'd gone for a walk in the Priory grounds, searching for mint to help with a patient's stomach pains. Eventually, she found some in a sheltered part of the gardens. It had been still, no one around, and Alice had sat on a stone bench and tried to find the peace which continued to evade her. But, as she allowed the stillness to surround her, she found no sense of peace, no soothing to be had. Instead, voices had popped into the silence. Voices and images—of William touching her hair, of William glancing at her with such heat that it took her breath away, and of William, the hurt in his eyes palpable as he watched her leave.

She shook her head and jumped up from the bench, trying to rid her mind and soul of images of him. But they refused to leave. Instead, others had been added: Katherine,

Lora, Celestria, laughing, their dramatic antics, steadiness, but above all, love, inhabiting the corners of her mind.

Her painful reveries were interrupted by the appearance of the Abbess's assistant with an invitation. Invitations to visit the Abbess were rarely received.

Alice wondered if someone else could be ill. She gathered her basket and herbs and hurried behind the nun. The Abbess wasn't used to being kept waiting.

Alice was escorted into the Abbess's private solar. The Abbess looked up from her work, and dismissed her secretary with a wave of the hand.

She waited until they were alone before offering Alice a seat by the fire, where some refreshments had been laid out. "Please take a seat and eat some of the cake. It is spiced with cinnamon and other spices brought from the East for me."

Alice didn't doubt it. It seemed the Abbess's contacts stretched all over the known world, and probably beyond that too.

"Thank you, my lady, but I am not hungry."

The Abbess shrugged and re-arranged her fine robes.

"And how have you settled in?" she asked, as she took a sip of her wine. "Well, I hope?"

Alice blinked. Few people were granted audiences with the Abbess, who was a powerful person, but, for some reason, the Abbess wanted to know something from her.

"The Priory is a beautiful, tranquil place, my lady. It would be a strange person who didn't settle in such surroundings." She hoped that would suffice the polite inquiry.

The Abbess grunted in a tone Alice couldn't comprehend. She looked at Alice and gave a brief smile. "You were ever a clever girl. When you used to come here as a little girl with your aunt, you couldn't get enough of our books and papers. You had a keen thirst for knowledge."

Alice felt her eyes light up at the memories of those happy days. "I'd never been anywhere where those were so many interesting things to learn."

"No, I daresay your family life wasn't very stimulating. And then, later." She gave Alice a perceptive glance. "You still couldn't get enough learning, but for different reasons. You wished to escape."

Alice swallowed. She hated talking about her past, but the Abbess was one of the only people who knew all of it. She'd had no choice at the time but to seek refuge there.

The Abbess leaned forward. "And that was what you needed at the time. But what I want to know, now, Alice, is if you're still seeking to escape. Because that is not why we are here. If you wish to live as a nun that is a positive choice, not a negative one. You must want this life with all your heart. Tell me what is in your heart."

"My heart…" Alice trailed off and looked away, unable to meet the Abbess's piercing gaze. She felt that, if she did, she wouldn't need to speak, that the Abbess would read the contents of her heart. She swallowed. "I cannot imagine living outside of here."

"That is not what I asked."

The silence lengthened as the Abbess patiently waited for a reply. It didn't look as if Alice was going to avoid answering the question honestly. She turned and met her gaze.

"My heart has been captured by a man."

"Sir William," prompted the Abbess.

"Yes."

"And so why are you here?"

"Because I am no match for him."

The Abbess steepled her fingers and tapped her lips. "In what way?"

"In every way."

"Is that why you lied to him?"

Alice looked up quickly and met the Abbess's perceptive stare. "What do you mean?"

"Exactly what I say. He told me that you'd said you did not love him."

Involuntarily, Alice drew her hands to her stomach and shook her head.

The Abbess narrowed her eyes. "Did you?"

Alice nodded. "I did."

"And why would you lie?"

"Because it was for the best."

"For him or for you."

"For him."

The Abbess sighed. "Excessive mortification is a sin, Alice. A sin before God and a sin before me."

"I did not intend it."

"But you did it nevertheless." Alice bit her lip and nodded. "And you truly think William is better off without you?"

"Aye, I do. All men want families, and I've known William for long enough to know that he wants one more than most. Growing up, he always spoke of it."

"That was a long time ago. Things change. People change."

"William doesn't. He's as unchanging as the land around him."

"You think that doesn't change?"

Alice looked up suddenly, caught by the difference in tone.

"If your William is as constant as you say he is, you may find that, like the land, what he grows, produces, rears, changes according to the season. It is winter now, but spring comes soon. A time for growth and renewal. For all of us." The Abbess reached out for Alice's hand. "Including you. You think you fear men now, but you too will change. Given nurturing conditions, you still have the tender buds which will grow and become strong again."

The Abbess's eyes held such warmth and sympathy, that Alice's eyes smarted.

"Now go, but you must think about what I've said. This is no place of escape, but a place to willingly choose to live that is not only for the benefit of all our lives and community here but for the benefit of the individual nuns. I would not have you be unhappy, Alice. You've suffered enough." She withdrew her hand. "I also have a task for you," she said, with a small tweak of the lips. "I have heard that there is sickness at Wanham Castle."

Alice leaped up, alarmed. "Sickness? What kind?"

"Not the plague. Be not alarmed. It is simply more of what we currently have here and that you are treating so effectively. But I would have you take your herbals and remedies and visit Wanham."

"Who is sick?"

"Katherine says her sister, Lora, is very sick."

Alice jumped up. "I will leave immediately." She made a mental note of what she needed. "No, I will first collect some remedies which I think will work more quickly than the others. And I will return by nightfall."

The Abbess shook her head. "It is a long way, and if you do that, you, yourself, will fall victim to the ague. No, I've sent word to Katherine that you will be staying a few nights. It is best, for everyone."

The Abbess was correct. By the time Alice and her servants were on the road, the dark skies had gathered iron-gray and angry overhead. Thunder rumbled in the distance, and jagged lightning filled the sky. It was not yet upon them but would be soon.

They quickened their pace and thus managed to reach the

gatehouse of Wanham Castle as large splashes of rain began to pelt down from the lowering, grumbling skies.

At a cry from the guard, Katherine came running out to greet her, a cloak held over her head for protection. They had to shout above the terrible rolls of thunder.

Alice looked around but saw no sign of William. Katherine gave her a quick hug, and they ran inside the Hall. A glance around the familiar home of only weeks before revealed everything to be in order. The dogs lay by the fire. The steward, Sir Harry, was at work on both the wine and the books. But there was no sign of the girls or William.

"They're upstairs," said Katherine, as if reading her thoughts. "In the bedchamber, where Lora lies."

"What are her symptoms?" Alice asked as she followed Katherine up the stone steps, which led to the girls' chambers.

"A dry cough and fever." She shook her head. "She's such a tomboy, out in all weathers. It was after a visit to Yarmouth that she fell sick. Goodness only knows who she'd been mixing with. She is as unaware of social niceties as Celestria, except in a completely different way. Anyway, I think she'll get well, but when I told the Abbess she insisted that you come over straight away. Of course, Celestria backed her up." Katherine opened the door and nearly stepped back—the heat of the room was intense after the cold outside.

Celestria released her sister's hand and jumped up to hug Alice. For all Celestria's dramatic ways, her heart was like gold, as was her loyalty. "Thank goodness you're here, Alice. I was afraid Lora would die if you didn't come."

Lora's eyelids flickered, revealing her agitation. "Lora won't die, Celestria!" said Katherine, after an anxious look at Lora. "But," she smiled at Alice, "she'll certainly recover more swiftly under Alice's care."

Alice placed her hand on Lora's forehead. It was hot but

not desperately so. She opened her bag and assembled her herbs.

After sponging Lora's face, Lora awoke and Alice gave her a drink, and she fell into an easier sleep.

Satisfied, Alice shooed everyone away, knowing they needed rest as much as Lora, and made herself at home. She had a feeling she wouldn't be leaving in a hurry.

A NIGHT and a day passed with Alice barely having left Lora's side, pressing warm cloths to her brow, and feeding her brews of herbs to bring out the fever. It wasn't until early evening of the second day that Lora's breathing became quieter. Alice felt her forehead and noted the fever had burned out. Lora fell into an easy sleep, and Alice left her in the care of a servant to give the news to the family.

Outside the bright sputtering fire and torch and candlelight of the Hall, a storm raged. But inside was a haven of peace. Katherine worked at a table by the fire, Celestria strummed a lute, while William talked with the steward. At another table, Warin and another squire played dice. Besides them, there was a constant flow of servants moving between the outbuildings and the Hall.

They all looked up as Alice entered the Hall. William jumped up and was beside her in an instant. He took her arm and brought her into the warmth of the fire and family circle. He poured her a cup of wine and bade her sit.

"How is Lora?" asked Katherine anxiously.

"The fever has broken," she said.

Sighs of relief were followed by muttered prayers and laughter. Celestria jumped up and ran upstairs to see Lora, despite Katherine's admonishment to leave her to sleep. William followed Celestria to the solar, leaving Alice alone with Katherine by the fireside.

"We've missed you, Alice," said Katherine over her piece of embroidery.

Alice felt heart-warmed by Katherine's comment. "I've only been gone a few weeks."

"But it felt like forever. We thought it would *be* forever."

Alice looked away quickly. "I must return to the Priory. I'm only here because you asked me to come for Lora's sake."

Katherine's brow gathered into a frown. "But…" She trailed off with a shrug.

"But what?"

"Surely it was the Abbess who said you wished to come to help Lora. I tried to tell her that she would be well shortly. But she said you insisted."

Alice's eyes widened with surprise. "I…" She swallowed. She couldn't bring herself to suggest that, for all her talk of truth, the Abbess had lied to return her to Wanham Castle. She shrugged and busied herself with her medicines.

She stilled as Katherine laid her hand upon her. "William was surprised you came."

She looked up but could think of nothing to say in return.

"I'm not sure he knew what to make of it," continued Katherine. "Nor do I, to be honest."

"I'm sorry to have given you such confusion. It was not my intention." She screwed up her face as she tried to work out how she could tell Katherine the truth without suggesting the Abbess had lied. She couldn't. "Please, tell me, how has William been? I thought he looked tired. Is he well?"

"When have you ever known William not to be well?"

It was an answer of sorts, but it told Alice nothing of what she wanted to hear. "Is he happy? I want him to be happy."

"There's only one way he'll ever be happy," said Katherine quietly. "And that's if you come back to him."

"Surely not, not after all I've said and done?"

Katherine didn't reply. She looked up suddenly and rose. "I'll leave him to answer that. I'll go check on Lora."

"Answer what?" asked William.

Alice thought quickly. "If you'd like some mulled wine."

Judging by William's expression, Alice wasn't sure she was believed, but he didn't question her further. Instead, he seemed content to sit with her and talk as friends, and gradually, she, too, relaxed. It was as if they had some kind of unspoken agreement that neither would talk of their feelings, but simply enjoy their time together.

By the end of the evening, the whole family, excepting Lora, was gathered by the fire, with the noise of the growing storm increasing outside the castle walls. Conversation was easy as they were all aware of her deafness. Katherine always spoke directly to her, knowing her problem with hearing, and Celestria spoke loudly anyway. Everything she said she seemed to declare as if it were of vital importance. She would have been good as one of the mummers if she'd been born into a different life, thought Alice with a smile. Her attention drifted as she imagined Celestria pacing the boards in a village. She would have loved it.

Suddenly there was a lull in the conversation as the evening drew to a close. It seemed no one wanted to leave the security of their small group to go to bed on that wild night.

Celestria suddenly shivered.

"You're not coming down with Lora's ailment, are you, Celestria?" asked Katherine in a worried voice.

Celestria shook her head and held up her finger in a dramatic gesture. "Listen!"

A silence descended, and they could hear the raging sea surge upon the shore, making the high tide even higher.

"I just pray," continued Celestria in a low, urgent voice, which sent corresponding shivers along everyone's backbones, "that there is no one out at sea this night. For it will be the worse for them."

Celestria had voiced what everyone else had been thinking.

Sir Harry took another sip of his wine. "The villagers might be hoping otherwise."

Katherine shot him an angry look. "Then they should not."

Sir Harry shrugged. "People need to eat."

"They have enough to eat," snapped Katherine, uncharacteristically.

"Katherine, Sir Harry is right," said William. "You cannot stop people lusting after things when they have so little."

"They have what they need. We make sure that none of our people go without."

"Going without is never enough for some people," said Sir Harry.

"Sir Harry speaks the truth, Katherine, whether we like it or not. Some of our people will be waiting for a tragedy this night so they can line their pockets."

Alice closed her eyes at the thought of greed on the back of such a disaster. "They would help the people aboard the ship, though?"

"Our people would. Or at least most of them wouldn't stand by and see a man drown. But while the people were recovering, guarded by some, others would be looting."

"But surely it is against the law."

"That it is. But many a lawman will turn his back in exchange for a barrel of port or some such."

"Then," said Alice, "let's pray that the seas rock no boats this night."

Katherine yawned and rose. "I must go to bed." She turned to Celestria, who was about to pour another cup of wine. "And so must you."

"But I—"

But even Celestria obeyed the look which Katherine gave her. Alice realized that Katherine had been a mother to her sisters in a way their mother hadn't. Sometimes she forgot how young Katherine was.

Katherine turned to Alice. "A bed is made up in the solar for you, Alice. Don't hurry back to the Priory." She glanced at William with a small smile and swept out of the Hall, making sure that Celestria came along with her. Sir Harry also got the hint and retired, leaving only the two of them.

William came and sat opposite her, by the fire. She looked at his dear face and saw suffering there that she'd never seen before. It was evident in the way he held his mouth, and in the deep line between his eyebrows. As if he were under siege, and he was doing all he could to repel the invader. She didn't want to be his enemy. She reached out and took his hand. She had no thought of doing so, her body moved of its own accord.

He looked up at her touch. "What are you doing?"

She shrugged but didn't move her hand. "Touching you. I..." She trailed off and tried to withdraw her hand, but he held it tightly. With his other hand, he cupped her cheek and swept his thumb across her lips. She gasped with surprise, and something more. It seemed he was awaiting her response as he immediately dipped his head to hers, paused, and then brushed her lips with his.

He drew away a hair's breadth from her face and slipped his hand around her head, supporting her neck. She could have moved, but the panic, which had always followed a physical advance upon her, wasn't there. Usually, it manifested itself in a constriction of the throat, a ringing in her ears, but she experienced none of this. She had no thought of withdrawal. The opposite, in fact. She wanted him closer, much closer.

In the end, it was Alice who pressed her lips against his, and for two heartbeats they stayed that way. Unfamiliar tingling sensations rippled through her body, opening up a world of feeling from which she'd previously been excluded.

When he opened his mouth against hers, she didn't pull away as his breath entered hers. Instead, she surrendered to the tender movement of his lips on hers, coaxing her to open her mouth to him. When she did, she gasped as heat flooded her body. It was as if her whole body was on fire, even though William did nothing further than caress her neck and kiss her.

It was as if sound bombarded her. As she relaxed in his arms, the noise in her ears, which was a constant companion in times of fear and stress, vanished. It was replaced by the sound of fire crackling in the grate and the whine of the wind outside as it rose in force, and the rain battering against the shutters.

It was only when he pulled away and looked toward the door that she realized that there was something more than the wind screaming. It was a guard, who'd come running from the gatehouse.

"A ship!" He stood before William, soaked to the bone. "A ship has foundered on the sands! All the villagers are there. You must come, Sir William, before any more people die!"

CHAPTER 10

William leaped to his feet, pulling on his cloak as he strode to the door.

"Alice! You must raise the girls. Tell them what's happened and that they're needed," said William as he opened the door, allowing a blast of cold air into the Hall. "I'll go on ahead. And you must come. You'll be needed too," he said.

She lit a lantern and handed it to him. The lantern swayed in the wind. Its light moved back and forth over his face, casting it one moment into shadow, the next into the lantern's yellow light, revealing the strength of his jawline and cheekbones. Whoever was in need that night, thought Alice, they couldn't ask for someone stronger or more determined than William to save them. And she lost her heart a little more to him.

She must have signaled something of her feelings in her eyes for he hesitated before plunging out into the maelstrom of the storm. Instead, he reached out and swept his thumb over her cheek in a brief caress. "And bring your bag of supplies. There will be injured people there."

"Of course," she said, smiling at his practical response while she'd been focused only on his touch against her skin. She held the door open for him. "Be safe, William." But he'd gone, running out into the wild night before he'd heard the words, her voice carried away on the whining wind.

Taking the stone steps two at a time, Alice dashed up to the bedchambers, her soaking dress dripping onto the floor.

Katherine shot bolt upright. "What is it? What's happened?"

"A ship has foundered on the beach." Alice gasped for breath. "William has gone ahead, but he needs all of our help."

Even before she finished speaking, Celestria was pulling on her clothes and racing out the door.

"Celestria! Wait! Don't be hasty!" called Katherine.

But it was too late, Celestria had reached the bottom of the stairs and was already opening the door to join the stream of people running to the beach.

Leaving Lora behind in bed, complaining bitterly at her weakened state, Katherine and Alice followed Celestria minutes later with their arms laden with the remainder of the mulled wine and spare cloaks with which to wrap the survivors.

When they struggled up the dunes with their loads, they stopped at the sight before them. There was no light from the stars or moon, only black sky, a black sea and the white tips of the waves which crashed upon the shore, illuminated by the swinging lanterns of the village folk who lined the beach, excitedly watching the drama unfold before them. Suddenly more people ran over the dunes toward the sea, raising darting lamps, further revealing the awful scene.

The prow of a boat was stuck up at a strange angle, high in the sea. And as the lights flickered over the scene, Alice saw people wriggling like worms as they clung to the side of the sinking boat and then fell into the raging sea, their screams lost in the screams of the wind.

A shout was raised, and she turned to see William, and other men, racing toward the sea. Then she heard Katherine gasp and followed her gaze out to the raging sea. The stern of the boat tipped into view before plunging back into the sea, where it was lost. This time when the waves parted, there was no sign of the boat, only a few bobbing heads in the water and raised arms as the survivors struggled to reach the shore.

There was chaos everywhere. People were running, dragging boats and ropes down to the sea. Some simply stood and watched, or sat on their haunches like birds of prey.

"Why are they not helping? They should help!" cried Alice.

Celestria, who was pulling on some breeches over her gown, glanced maliciously at the people. "They have no thought of help. Only of plunder." She scanned their faces. "I know who they are! And they will regret their lack of humanity."

Then suddenly Celestria raced off.

"What is she doing?" shouted Alice above the noise of the wind and waves "Katherine! We should stop her!"

"She cannot be stopped. The Lord himself wouldn't be able to stop Celestria. If Mother couldn't, no one can." Katherine placed a comforting hand on Alice. "Do not worry. Celestria can look after herself." She paused, and a strong gust of wind pushed them both back a step. "I hope," she added grimly, as they watched her climb aboard a boat which was launched into the raging sea. "She can swim like a fish. Besides, she knows these waters well. Where the rocks are, where the eddies are. God willing, she'll be safe."

But then Alice lost all thought of Celestria as William, a rope securely tied around him, plunged into the sea. He quickly drove through the sea and came across a couple of dark patches, which he grasped before calling out. He was hauled back to shore, his arms securely around two people who began to thrash and nearly drowned them all until his instructions calmed them.

Once brought to shore, Alice and Katherine pulled the half-drowned people to one side and worked on them. They were sick in the sand. It was a father and boy. They rolled over, and after coughing the women realized they would be well and passed them to a villager who had clothing and hot soup for them.

Alice pulled her cloak around her and peered out into the darkness. Celestria's boat, pulled by two strong men, was closest to the upended boat now.

William pulled more people out of the sea and brought them to shore. They were a woman and a small child. They were in a worse way than the others and immediately Alice could see the child had died. But the woman, whose lungs rattled, continued to hold the child to her side.

Alice made her as comfortable as she could in the howling gale, sheltered by a large sand dune, and tried to lift the woman. It seemed she hadn't drowned as there was no water coming from her mouth. But as Alice eased her up in her arms, she saw the pool of blood coming from her head. While the daughter had drowned, the mother was dying from a fatal blow to the head.

The mother's eyes fluttered open. And she made a sound which could have been a name, or simply a gasp. "Cha—" the woman said. She tried to look around, and Alice hushed her.

"Please do not move. You're bleeding."

The woman moved her head regardless, rolling it back and forward. "Cha—" she said, exhaling with all her might.

Alice didn't know what she was trying to say. "Cha?" she asked.

The woman licked her lips. "Charles," she said. "My baby." The word 'baby' seemed to revive her. She dug her fingertips into Alice's arm. "Where is he?"

Alice shook her head. "I don't know." The woman's eyes creased in pain. "But William will get him." She turned to see William bringing in a small bundle, wading through the high waves unaided, his eyes focused in the distance. "I think he has him," said Alice, risking the guess to comfort the woman. Then she saw William hold up the bundle, and a piercing baby's cry filled the air. "Bless the Lord! I do believe it is." She cried out loud. "He's safe! Charles is—" Then she turned to the woman who now lay lifeless on the blood-soaked sand, her young child still in her arms. Alice's cry changed to a wail.

She signaled William over to her, and he placed the small screaming baby into Alice's arms. Immediately Alice brought her cloak around the child.

"Most of the crew was rescued," he said, nodding toward Celestria's boat, which was being maneuvered to shore, full of men. "But the family had taken refuge beneath deck, and were the first to go. He shook his head as he looked down at the dead woman and girl. "One of the men said they were the only family onboard. She was a widow traveling to a new life somewhere. He knew not her name, nor her destination, nor anything else about her. He looked at the baby. "It seems this baby is all that remains of the family. And it's nameless."

"It's not an 'it'," said Alice. "It's a he, and his name is Charles." She looked up at William with tears in her eyes. "She was asking after him before she passed away." Alice made the sign of the cross and nestled the baby closer to her. The baby's cries lessened.

William put his arm around her and pushed the cloth away from the baby's face. Despite its cries, it was deathly white. “Go.” He looked around and beckoned Katherine over. “Both of you return to the castle and look after the babe.”

Alice didn’t need telling twice and was already hurrying across the wet sands to the dunes, which would lead her back to the road to the castle. Despite the short distance, it seemed to take an age, and by the time they had entered the Hall, she was wet to the skin and shivering from the rain and from pressing the soaking bundle of Charles to her chest.

She called to the maid. “Go warm some milk.” She awkwardly pulled off her cloak and peeled away the wet layers. “And some dry clothes to swaddle the babe in!”

Alice plucked a fur mantle from a hook and lay it before the fire where she placed the babe. He immediately began to scream, his arms and legs flailing as she struggled to unwrap him from his soaking clothes. Her usual control was shattered as she tried to focus on peeling off his clothes and getting him warm and dry. Her hands were shaking by the time he lay naked on a warm, dry cloth. She had no time to admire his pale skin, but quickly wrapped him in some clothes the maid had brought. She held the babe close to her body, snuggled into her arms, and rocked him. It was only then that the baby quieted.

The maid looked up at her with open curiosity on her face. Alice, herself, had no idea where the impulse had come from, that the baby needed closeness above all else. No idea that she could rock to soothe someone else held so close to her. She had no memory of ever holding a babe in her arms before. That something so natural still existed deep within her surprised her. She kissed the baby’s downy head before slipping on a cap which the maid offered. With the seawater smell of the babe still fresh on her lips, she pulled him against her once more.

“The babe is quiet in your arms. It’s as if he knows you.”

Alice caught the maid’s wondering glance and shook her

head. “How could he?” She stroked his downy head. “All he knows is what my arms are telling him. That he’s safe and loved.” The words slipped out of her unawares. It was only after she’d said them that she realized they were true, spoken from the heart—a heart she hadn’t known to be still alive in her previously frozen body.

She took the cup of warmed milk from the maid. “What’s this?” asked Alice, puzzling over what looked like a piece of fine animal skin fashioned into a small cone shape, with a small mesh-covered cut in its end.

“It’ll aid the babe’s feeding. My old mam used to use one for her grand-babies when there was no one to feed them. Do it like this,” said the maid, carefully pouring a little milk into the cloth and guiding Alice’s hand to the babe’s mouth, which was open, as were his eyes. He immediately latched onto the thing which spluttered out the milk. And for one moment, she thought the babe would drown in milk rather than the sea, but then the maid adjusted the flow, and the babe suckled deeply. Even when the milk had gone, and the babe’s eyes were closed, his mouth continued to suckle. When the maid took away the milk, Alice gave the babe her little finger to suckle instead, and he settled once more.

As the cries and shouts outside grew louder, Alice took him upstairs to a small solar where they wouldn’t be disturbed. As the wind raged around the castle, Alice sang lullabies she thought she’d forgotten to the babe. Alice was aware of the people’s shouts as they brought the survivors into the Hall, and revived them with dry clothes, food, and wine. The dead would also be cared for. William would make sure of that. But she had her arms full, and her heart, as she focused on the infant who lay fast asleep against her body. She couldn’t take her eyes off him. Such a scrap to be left so alone. Except he wasn’t alone, was he? He had her. And she vowed, there and then, that she'd never fail him. She'd make sure he'd never be alone in the world again.

And so the night deepened as life continued outside the walls of the solar, the dead were cared for, the living revived, and the world returned to normal. Except nothing was as it had been before for Alice. This tiny baby had reached deep inside of her and found a place within her, which she hadn't known to exist.

Alice was filled with sorrow that his mother and sister had died in the tragedy. But with their death, it was as if she'd been brought to life.

MUCH LATER, William was able to leave the Hall, now full of sleeping people who'd been rescued from the ship. As he made his way to Alice's solar, he tried to forget the haunting image of the woman who lay, her young daughter still in her arms, beneath a sheet in an outbuilding.

He knocked quietly on the solar door, but receiving no answer, he pushed it open. He was about to speak but the words melted at the sight which greeted him. Alice didn't look up. The firelight flickered around her, giving an orange glow to her usually cool blonde features. He couldn't see the babe, and it made no sound. Only its bulky swaddling was visible, peeping out from Alice's cloak as she gazed, motionless, to where the babe's face must be.

She looked up suddenly, and the light in her eyes lit a corresponding one in his heart.

"William," she breathed. "Charles is asleep." William walked over to them, and she eased the baby from her chest and showed him. "Isn't he beautiful?"

William had little knowledge of babies. And this one didn't seem particularly beautiful to him. He was tiny, fair with a snub nose and rosy lips. He cleared his throat. "Beautiful," he repeated, hoping that would suffice. But then he looked at Alice and repeated the word, knowing she wouldn't realize that he meant her. "Beautiful." He pushed away a strand of hair that had fallen across her face. He had a strange feeling as she looked up at him again with a smile. He'd never seen that expression before. Something inside of her had been ignited. Something glowed. He almost had a stab of jealousy. But then she raised her hand to his cheek and caressed him, and he leaned into her caress.

"He's our miracle, William. He's my baby now." Without waiting for an answer, Alice brought Charles against her body and leaned back with a sigh and closed her eyes.

William took a step away, struck by a myriad of thoughts that made no sense. He was happy that Alice was happy. But her words struck him like a blow. She'd said "my baby". It appeared that the baby was an orphan, but that Alice should so swiftly take to the baby astonished him.

He was about to move away when he heard her say something else. He couldn't believe his ears. "What did you say?"

"*Our* baby, William." She smiled sleepily before her eyes closed once more. "Our baby. With him in our lives, we could do as you wanted. We could marry because he could be our future. Our family."

He swallowed, looked at them both, and for the first time in a long time, hope was alight in his heart.

CHAPTER 11

When Alice opened the shutters the next morning, her first thought as she looked across the fields toward the sea was that there had been no storm the night before. The sky was a bright blue, as if newly washed, and the air smelled of salt and earth—the two things she always thought of when it came to Wanham, and William. It was only when she lowered her gaze to the surrounding fields and castle bailey that she saw the havoc that the storm had wrought.

Tree branches lay scattered around the fields and lane which led toward the river, and thatch from the outbuildings now lay over everything, turning the courtyard and road into a field of broken reeds. But it was the number of people who clustered in the bailey, which drew her attention. The sun had not yet risen and yet there were people everywhere, caring for the survivors. William was talking with a group of people she didn't recognize. She was concerned by their grim looks and seriousness of manner, and she resolved to find out what was wrong. But there were other demands on her time before she discovered what was amiss with William.

A grizzling sound caught her attention, and she saw Charles had suddenly awoken, disturbed by the absence of her body, and was demanding either food or attention. Whichever it was, she'd make sure he received it.

She took the cup with the soft spout attached and angled it towards Charles. It took a few messy moments to get the flow right, but he was hungry. He didn't appear too fussed by the unusual way he was receiving his food or bothered by the difference between the goat's milk and his mother's.

Once Charles had been satisfied, Alice quickly dressed and wrapped him in a warm fur wrap and went downstairs. But she was not on her way to William. Instead, she passed through the Hall, which was crowded with the rescued men who appeared much improved by William's generosity. The Hall was as busy as the courtyard. While the castle's steward, Sir Harry, was busy with William and the officials, Katherine and Celestria were doing what each did best—giving comfort by organizing the victuals and entertaining people with tall tales.

But Alice didn't linger in the Hall. Once in the courtyard, she made a few inquiries, and made her way to the farthest corner, where a small storeroom stood. The door was closed, and she pushed it open. It took a little while for her eyes to become accustomed to the gloom inside. Then she saw her—Charles's mother, her body covered from top to toe, and next to her the smaller body of her child.

Part of Alice wanted to retreat, to return to the people and noise of the bailey and the Hall. But she owed it to both Charles and his mother—the woman who'd died with her baby's name on her lips.

She swallowed her fears and, drawing the babe tighter against her, went to where the two bodies lay. She hesitated, nervous at what she'd see beneath the sheet. She took a deep breath and pulled it away. Apart from a waxy white, their faces were unharmed, and they could have been sleeping. Someone had bound the mother's head for appearance's sake, to hide the gash, but her child's face was untouched.

"Look, Charles," she said, turning the baby toward the bodies. His eyes blinked as if recognizing his name and he looked down at the bodies. "It's your mother," she whispered between dry lips. "And your sister."

The baby whimpered slightly, and Alice thought she might have made a mistake. The baby reached out, and Alice's heart clenched. Then the baby stopped and looked around in confusion. It was as if he recognized the form, but knew that that form was missing a vital element.

"They're no longer with us, Charles," said Alice, repeating his name, which he seemed to know. He swung his head to look at Alice again and gave a small, uncertain smile. "But you must know they loved you and cared for you your whole life up till now. And now it's my turn. And I promise I will not fail you."

She laid her hand on the mother's hands as a gesture of reassurance. "I promise," she repeated, except this time to the mother.

She did the same to the dead child. "God bless." She gave the sign of the cross and murmured a blessing before covering them both. She shivered then and, wiping away a tear, she stepped out into the fresh chill of the dawn air. She glanced down at the baby in her arms, whose eyes watched her every move, as if uncertain about her. She smiled reassuringly and received a smile that was tentative at first but then suddenly blossomed into a grin and a gurgle, along with a little milk that smeared his lips. She laughed and heard someone call her name.

She looked up to see William smiling at her. He walked over. "It's good to see you happy." He pushed the covers away from the baby's cheeks, and his smile broadened. "He's a bonny boy, that's for sure, and he looks like he's happy to be in your arms." William looked up and caught her eye. "And who wouldn't be?"

William didn't usually talk like this, and the cheekiness of his comment made her burst out in laughter. Katherine passed by and grinned. It seems laughing and smiling wasn't something people usually heard from Alice. She hadn't even realized it.

William glanced across at the men who he'd been talking to earlier, who appeared intent on talking to everyone in the bailey yard. All signs of humor had gone.

"Who are those men, William?"

"They're from the magistrates' court." His lips thinned. "They're here about the looting. Looking for men to prosecute."

"But surely they won't find any? You made sure of that."

"I certainly tried to," he said. "But there are those who were too quick, and who disappeared into the darkness before I could reach them."

"Do you know of these men? Do *they*?"

"Aye, I do. But they do not." His lips set grimly. "Not yet. And I pray to God that their bribes do not work on the others to reveal their names."

"Why, what would happen?"

"They would be taken to court, found guilty, and hung."

"Then surely no one will inform, will they?"

William shrugged. "The harvest was good, our people have food, but for some of the larger families, there's never enough. Try to get a man to pass up on a barrel of brandy when he's been drinking weak ale all his life." He shook his head. "They are poor men, Alice, and used to taking advantage whenever they can. They think of it as a gift from the sea."

"Not a view the magistrates share," murmured Alice.

"Indeed not. And they hold me responsible, so it is up to me to make sure our men are not discovered. Go inside, Alice, and keep yourself and the babe warm. The owner of the vessel has information on the people sailing in it. I'll find out all I can."

Alice pulled the little bundle closer to her chest and knew that she'd already lost her heart to the babe. And that it would break it if she had to let him go.

"I'm sorry, Alice, but there's still a possibility that the babe has family who wishes to take him in. You must be prepared for that."

She couldn't bring herself to speak because she knew that she was quite unprepared for that. But she'd make herself do whatever she had to do. Hadn't she always?

"But, while we try to trace the relatives, the babe can stay at Wanham in your care. The magistrates agree. It's one less problem for them to worry about."

They both looked down at the sleeping babe. She tried to smile at William but failed. "You must go and work with the magistrates. Your people need you."

"Aye." He squeezed her arm and returned to the group of men, where the voices were already becoming raised. Sir Harry was trying to calm them. He'd been playing for time.

Alice returned inside the Hall, and Katherine immediately called to her. Reluctantly Alice surrendered the sleeping babe to her maid and went and checked on one particular patient, who was now delirious.

Alice dropped to her knees. "But he seemed all right when we went to bed."

"He's just started acting like this."

Alice quickly checked and found that a wound was deeper than they'd first thought. She shook her head at Katherine, who crossed herself.

"All we can do is make him comfortable," said Alice.

She gave him a potion of hemlock to try to make him unaware of what was going on, and then sat back and cuddled Charles.

It wasn't until the sun had risen in the guileless sky that it shone upon the face of the man, which no longer moved. The servants removed the body, and Alice turned her attention to Celestria, who'd just entered the Hall and who paced, back and forth, before the fire.

Celestria swept her arm in the general direction of the village. "They've all gone there to find any looters. Not that they will. By God's teeth, I hope they don't! I know they won't!"

"Celestria!" admonished Katherine. Alice wasn't sure if Katherine was more shocked by Celestria's swearing or by the fact Celestria appeared to know something about the looting.

Celestria ignored her elder sister and paused mid-pace and tapped her fist against her lips. "No, they won't catch anyone."

Katherine tilted her head in inquiry. "How can you be so certain?"

For the first time, Celestria looked up at her and gave a quick smile. "You know me, Katherine, I'm certain of everything!"

Katherine and Alice watched Celestria stride out of the room, and then run up the stairs. "She has a hand in it," said Katherine blankly. "She might be against them looting but she'll defend her people to the death." She blinked and turned a frowning face to Alice. "Alice, what am I to do? Celestria is impossible!"

Alice shifted the babe so that he lay against her shoulder and put her arm around Katherine. "You've done all you can do for her. You've given her guidance, and the rest is up to her."

Katherine watched Celestria burst through the door with her cloak flying behind her and run outside. "And I have a feeling Celestria hasn't taken to heart my guidance. If there's a drama anywhere, she'll be in the midst of it." She gnawed her lip. "I'll have Warin go after her."

Katherine went in search of Warin, leaving Alice and the baby. She sat by the crackling fire, an oasis of calm as maids and men worked around her. She wasn't needed anywhere else, so enjoyed her time playing with Charles, discovering his personality, and marveling at his beauty.

It wasn't until late afternoon that William returned.

Alice looked up immediately. He caught her gaze and turned away to toss aside his cloak. She poured him a glass of wine and brought him some left-over victuals from their morning meal.

He took a swig of much-needed wine and then looked at her thoughtfully. "How are you and the babe?"

"Charles is very good, very placid, so long as he eats regularly."

William laughed. "A typical boy, then." His laughter faded as he caught her hand in his. "And you? You've told me naught about how you fare."

Alice shrugged. "There's little to tell. I've helped where I can and been caring for Charles. There's a lot to learn."

"I'm sure. But you seem to have adapted quickly. He looks content." When she looked up, he caught her gaze. "As do you. More so than I've ever seen you before."

She glanced around. The place was full of people, and she didn't want to divulge to everyone just *how* different caring for Charles had made her feel. It was like a shell had been broken from around her. She seemed more aware of William, of his feelings and thoughts, of the girls, of everyone. It was as if color had suddenly come into her life. And she realized how much she'd cut herself off from feeling. Well, the shell had broken, whether she liked it or not. Allowing in good things, and no doubt, bad things. But there was nothing bad around her at the moment, nothing that could hurt her. On the contrary. But that was for a later conversation when they were alone.

"Please, tell me how you fared today, William. Did you satisfy the justices?"

He smiled as if he realized what she was doing. "There were two men I suspected had taken off with booty from last night's storm. And I tried to delay—it would have fallen bad on their families, as well as us—but the men must have been tipped off. For when we reached their homes, neither of them were to be found."

"That was lucky."

"I doubt luck had much to do with it." He looked around. "What time did Celestria return?"

She frowned. "Late. Why?"

He sighed and placed his cup on the table. "Because I found Celestria at the last house we went to."

Alice gasped. "Did the justices recognize her?"

"I don't think so. She raised her hood and slipped past me. Acting like a quiet, demure, innocent girl." He huffed. "A new role for her."

"Do you think she had a hand in this?"

"Most certainly. She went ahead of us and tipped them off. No doubt gave them the funds with which to disappear."

"So they're safe."

"And we're safe. Thanks to Celestria and her love for drama."

"But she also has a good heart. She did what she did to protect your people."

"Aye, it is true. But there's a big part of me that wished she didn't. She's my sister, and the scrapes she's getting herself into are getting bigger and bigger. I fear that one day…"

He trailed off, but Alice knew what he feared. For it was the same as she did. One day Celestria would take a step too far, and it would be the worse for her.

"You cannot know. Mayhap…"

"Mayhap, it might not come to pass. But most likely, it will." He finished eating. "Now, tell me about your day. How was the babe?"

"A little unsettled, but I've held him close all morning."

He smiled and nodded. "Don't get too close, Alice. He may be claimed yet." Their gaze met and held a world within it. He rose. "Come, join me in the solar. I would have a little privacy."

She checked on Charles, who was still sleeping in the cot beside the fire, attended by the maid and Lora.

William stepped aside, and she entered the empty room first. Then she heard him close the door and they were alone.

He came close to her, but she didn't step away, simply raised her face to his with a smile. She had a feeling she knew what he was about to do, and, for once, she wasn't of a mind to deny him.

He raised his hand to her face and gently ran the back of his fingers down her cheek. "You are so beautiful."

She opened her mouth to speak, but before she could utter a sound, his mouth had claimed hers in a kiss as powerful as it was surprising.

There could be no doubt that his kiss was possessive, something which she'd always feared, but it wasn't fear which was making her move her hands around him, holding him firm where he could explore her lips. He gasped and pulled away.

"I'm sorry, I should not have done that. I—"

"William!"

"It was overly familiar. Too soon. It was—"

"Exactly right. William, can you not feel my hands still

gripping you? Not wanting you to move away? You're right, something in me has changed. I'm not afraid to feel anymore."

But before he could answer, Katherine knocked on the door and looked from one to the other of them. "I'm sorry, Alice, but Charles has awoken, and we can't seem to comfort him like you do."

Alice rushed into the Hall where she picked up the wailing Charles and held him close. She didn't jiggle him as she'd seen others do but held him steady, and his cries soon turned into quiet hiccups.

"You have a way with him, that's for sure," said Lora, watching her astutely. "But what's going to happen to him when he leaves here?"

"He won't leave here," said Katherine. "Not unless a close relative turns up out of the blue, and it doesn't seem there are any. No, I think it's clear. Who better to look after him than Alice?"

"Maybe someone who's married?" suggested Sir Harry, looking scandalized at the prospect of an unmarried woman taking on someone else's baby.

They all looked at William. "Aye, you're right, Sir Harry," said William. "Whoever cares for Charles should be married."

Alice gasped. She couldn't believe William would take the babe from her.

He cleared his throat, and before them all dropped to one knee. "Lady Alice de Courcy, I'm offering you my hand in marriage. Will you accept?"

Alice couldn't believe her ears. The whoops and cheers of the crowded Hall receded into a dull roar. All she could see was William kneeling before her, his eyes fixed on her, and all she was aware of was the lack of any word of love. But it was William, and it was Charles.

"Come on, Alice!" yelled Celestria, so loudly, she couldn't help but hear. "What do you say?"

Alice licked her lips, her heart pounding, tight in her chest. Could she do this? Could she pledge herself to William after everything that had happened, after so many years of resigning herself to spinsterhood?

"Please, Alice," said Katherine, half-laughing, half in despair, "don't keep me guessing. I cannot stand it."

Charles gurgled in her arms. She looked down, and he smiled at her. She smiled back and lifted her face to William.

"Aye, I will."

CHAPTER 12

The uproar pulsed in Alice's ears, but she didn't look around. Someone took the baby from her arms, and she held William's stunned gaze. She wondered if he'd heard her, but before she could repeat the words, a look of joy spread across his face, and he beamed.

"Yes!" he said, as he gripped Alice by the waist and twirled her around. She cried out in surprise but was set back on her feet before she knew where she was. She reached out for William to steady herself, and he pulled her into his arms. "Yes!" he repeated, and this time he kissed her in front of everyone.

The shock was quickly followed by a weakening in her limbs, which made her grasp him even tighter. She was beginning to be oblivious to her surroundings, aware only of his kiss when he pulled away, and with a sigh set her back on her feet. He held one hand tightly as he looked around at his family. "She said yes!"

"Of course she did, Will!" said Celestria, hugging Alice. "Why wouldn't she?"

Katherine smiled at Alice, knowing full well why she

might have said "no". "Indeed, Will, do you doubt your charms?"

"Aye," he said, squeezing Alice's hand. "I have none. I am what I am. And I feared it wasn't enough."

All through these exchanges, Alice's mind was numb. The words of the proposal and her response tracked over and over until she began to believe them.

His last words broke the spell. "You are *more* than I deserve, William."

"Nay, lass, don't ever think that," he said, huskily.

Lora made a puking noise behind them. "I don't know what all the fuss is about. I'm never going to get married."

"Then more fool you," said Celestria. "I'm going to marry someone rich and powerful and exciting, and have a wonderful life."

"If you marry someone rich and powerful and exciting, you'll have *no* life. You'll be tied to them, forced to do whatever they're doing, following their orders," retorted Lora.

Katherine choked on her laughter. "Celestria, following orders? I'd like to see that."

"You will if she marries someone rich and powerful and exciting," said Lora.

"You do what you want. Katherine will no doubt marry someone dull and worthy, and Lora can be an outlaw if she chooses, but I know what I want. And, today, I want to plan your wedding, Alice. May I?"

Alice had been vaguely listening to the chatter, glad of it because it diverted the attention from her and William, who continued to hold her hand fast. He'd said nothing about love, she reminded herself. Mayhap it was merely the child and his strong sense of loyalty which had prompted the proposal. Mayhap her disclosure of her past had soured his interest in her.

"Can I?" repeated Celestria. "Can I arrange your wedding feast?"

Alice forced herself to attend. She gave a quick smile. "Aye, if you like."

Celestria shrieked and clapped her hands. "We'll invite everyone, there will be music and dancing—"

Alice exchanged a glance with Katherine.

"I think Alice would prefer something more dignified than that!" said Katherine. "We will do it together." She nodded to Alice, who was reassured that Katherine would be able to curb Celestria's excesses. But no matter, she knew that with Celestria's input, it would be fun.

"When will it happen?" asked Katherine.

"The sooner, the better," said William.

The rest of the day was spent in speculation about the wedding feast by the sisters, while William's men insisted on celebrating by raiding the castle's wine stores. Alice could scarcely believe it had happened. As each hour passed, with the babe asleep, Alice's fears grew once more. What had she agreed to? She loved William as a friend, but she'd be *more* than a friend. She'd have to lie with him in his bed. His kisses had been persuasive, but she knew, from bitter experience, that there was a lot more to a relationship than a kiss. After what she'd been subjected to, she didn't know how she'd react to his advances. And, if she did accept them, would the act change her feelings toward him?

Should she change her mind? The thought of its impact on Charles, as well as William's sisters, would have been enough to stop her from changing her mind, without the knowledge of how much it would hurt William. But she did need to voice her fears.

When the maid informed Alice that Charles was crying and couldn't be comforted, she was pleased to be able to go to him. The excited women continued to talk of weddings, and William stoically endured the butt of jokes from his men.

It seemed Charles had some kind of teething problem, and after rubbing some herbal ointment onto his gums, it took Alice some time to settle him.

Eventually, she slept beside him. It was a creak in the floorboards which alerted her to someone else's presence. She flickered open her eyelids, checked on Charles, who lay sleeping peacefully now, the redness in his cheeks abated and his breathing even. Then a shadow moved. She started.

"It is only me," said William, coming forward into the light of the fire.

"Oh, you startled me."

"I knocked, but there was no response, and I wanted to make sure you were all right."

Alice slid her feet onto the floor and pushed her hair out of her face. "I've been asleep. Charles is teething."

William came and looked down at him. "He looks peaceful now."

"I gave him something for the discomfort, and he eventually quieted. It'll pass in a few days."

She rose, and they both looked down at the sleeping babe. Alice suddenly felt uncomfortable, aware of the intimacy of the situation. Gently, she scooped up Charles and laid him in the cot. This time, he didn't murmur, but continued to sleep, exhausted by his earlier outburst.

"You have a way with that babe, Alice," said William, coming to her side.

She continued to look at Charles. "I think it's the other way around. He has a way with me. I feel different when I'm with him. As if I'm doing what I'm meant to do, for the first time in my life."

William didn't reply, and eventually, Alice turned to him to see tears in his eyes.

"My heart aches for you, Alice. I wish I could turn back time and prevent what happened to you, but I can't. All I can do is be here for you now, and promise you that I'll never hurt you."

"I know, William. You are a good man. But..." How could she explain her fears?

"But what?"

"I know you have no wish to hurt me. But it doesn't stop me from being afraid. And when I'm scared, it's as if winter has come to my soul. As if the heat of my body has leached away, as if..." She hesitated and closed her eyes as she tried to find the words to describe how she felt. She opened her eyes. "As if I've become a block of ice."

As if to underline her words, a slice of silver moonlight shone across the floor from a crack in the shutters. It seemed to chill and flicker the rosy glow from the candle, which was all but sputtering now, having been lit hours earlier.

"Just as well then, that I know what to do with ice." William pushed her hair from her face and cupped her cheeks gently as if framing a picture. A little of the ice melted.

"What do you do with ice?" she asked, knowing, but wanting to engage at some flirtatious level she didn't understand.

His lips twitched briefly. "Different things, depending on what is frozen. If, say, the land was frozen, and it was dawn, then I would wait for nature to do its work and for the soil to soften until it could be managed. Patience is what's required in that case."

"But what if the temperature didn't rise enough to melt the ice? What if it continued to be hard and unyielding through the dark day and into the night when it froze even harder?" The constriction in her throat was betrayed by her voice. Panic, she thought, was hard to disguise.

"Well, that depends on how much we're talking about. If it were a small patch that was precious, then I would protect it."

"Not dig it up?"

"No, that isn't the best way. Attack is rarely the best way with the land. Nurture always pays dividends. The best way to protect it from the elements is to cover it with cloth and shelter, so it receives no more damage. To help it come alive by itself. That is the best way. Or else, there may be pockets still frozen, lying unseen. No doubt."

"Ah," she breathed. "No doubt," she repeated, swaying a little toward him, aware of strange tingles running down her back, along her limbs, turning them liquid.

He brushed his thumb against her lips. "And if the cloths and shelter didn't work, then I would use myself as protection, lie on it to warm it, breathe on it, like I would a resisting lock until the key turned easily. That is what I would do."

This time she couldn't even begin to form any words, just held herself close to him, her mouth but a whisper away from his, feeling his breath against her mouth.

Did she move first, or did he? She couldn't have said, but their lips met and touched and held, as if he were breathing life into her, melting her reserve, filling her with goodness so she could trust again.

Her heart thumped heavily, and her body was flooded with heat which seemed to do exactly as he'd described, melted her from top to toe. She could have pulled away easily, but she didn't. It was as if he'd been testing her, to see her response, and when she didn't reject him, he moved his lips over hers slowly. She didn't know that lips could be caressed like that. The warmth of his breath in her mouth was a further intoxication. She felt his groan, deep in his body, rumble through hers as he stepped closer until their bodies touched, and his hands slid around her back, fanning over her, supporting her.

She heard a whimper and realized that it came from her.

Too soon, he pulled away. A slow smile spread over his face as he swept her lower lip with his thumb. "You, my love, have nothing to fear."

His words struck her, not only because of their meaning, but because they claimed her hearing, loud and clear. She shook her head in confusion. He frowned and held her more firmly.

"What is it?"

But she couldn't answer because she was suddenly aware of the sound of an owl, hooting outside the window. She turned to look at the window where the moon shone strongly now.

"Did you hear that?"

He frowned. "What? The owl? Of course." Then his frown cleared. "Why, did you?"

She nodded and walked to the window and swung open the shutters. A blast of cold air entered the room. Moonlight flooded the land, giving it an unnatural silver light, revealing the damage the storm had wrought only the day before. Nothing stirred.

He came up behind her and held her shoulders. "There'll be a heavy frost tomorrow."

The sound of the owl broke through the silence, and Alice closed her eyes. "I've never heard an owl like that before. Not so clear. I can hear the texture of the call, the feeling behind it. But this is not a numb, faint sound, but a full one."

"I don't understand," said William. "What could have happened to change your hearing?"

She twisted in his arms and smiled up at him. "The ice breaking a little, mayhap?"

A rare grin broke across his face. “Mayhap. And imagine what magic more loving can bring.”

More loving. There was no doubt she’d enjoyed the kiss. But simply the mention of the physical act which would inevitably be expected of her clamped something tight within her. She felt the old tension fall over her again, like a protective cloak—a smothering cloak which triggered something inside of her, blanking out the sounds as before.

William must have sensed the tension return to her body, for his smile fell like a stone. But his hands didn’t leave her, only relaxed their hold. “You know that a miracle has happened, and it can happen again. I swear to almighty God that I will help you. I will show you a little each day that there is nothing to fear from our union. It has begun with a kiss, and I promise you many more of those. And then? We will take it slowly, so slowly that your fear will leave you, and the demands of your body will outgrow your fears. That, my dear Alice, is my promise to you. A future where there is no fear, only love.”

She couldn’t believe it, although she wanted to. She put her arms around him and pressed her cheek to his chest. His arms wrapped tightly around her, and there they stayed, bathed in the cool moonlight until a small gurgle came from the cot. They both turned to see the light had awoken Charles, who lay happily watching them both.

As Alice walked to the cot, she heard William murmur. “With every day that passes, Alice de Courcy, I’ll show you how much I love you. I’ll make sure you don’t ever forget it.”

As if she wanted to. It was the one thing she’d valued her whole life, and because of that, it was the one thing that scared her.

But William didn’t have the opportunity to show her how

much he loved her over the following weeks. Because, as the last weeks of winter passed into spring, the country was sent into a state of alarm by news from the King. Especially for those living on the coast. Philip Augustus, King of France, fresh from taking Normandy from the King of England, King John, now appeared to have his sights set on England itself. Word had reached King John that his old allies, now allies of the French King, had joined forces with Philip Augustus and were planning to invade England. All ports and coastal areas were put on alert. Every male over the age of twelve had to bear arms, and all ships had been requisitioned by the King to defend the realm.

What this meant for William was intensive organization to make sure that his coastline was guarded, that there were sufficient men or women to work the land, and that the trade, which had fallen mostly to Katherine, was able to continue in some form. Luckily the difficult Captain who seemed to be the bane of Katherine's life also managed to avoid his ship being controlled by the King. On the one hand, this meant their trade could continue and prosper, but on the other, it meant more difficulty for Katherine in managing the Captain—a man who they continued to hear plenty of.

"He's impossible!" said Katherine, pacing the room in a way she never did unless Captain Logan had upset her again. "He does the opposite of what I say. He seems intent on goading me into anger. Only then does he laugh and do what he wants anyway. Which, it has to be said, often seems to work out better than I had anticipated." She threw her arms in the air. "He's impossible!" she repeated.

"You've already said that," noted Lora, wryly.

"For someone who purports to dislike this man, you seem to spend a lot of time talking about him. I think you're sweet on him," said Celestria.

Alice couldn't help thinking she might have a point, but

now, she decided, wasn't a time to question Katherine, whose face had grown puce with anger.

"I'm indifferent to him!" said Katherine, with too much passion.

"It's unlikely, Celestria," said Alice, mildly. Unlikely though possible, she thought.

"Unlikely? It's impossible!" Katherine turned away, but not before Alice thought she saw tears in her eyes. Whether they were tears of frustration or anger, she didn't know. What she *did* know was that they weren't tears of indifference. Katherine stormed off, and the girls drifted away, each in pursuit of their different interests: for Katherine, domestic matters, for Lora, William's work, and Celestria… Alice didn't even want to think where Celestria might be.

Alice settled beside the fire with Charles. The weeks had passed and, despite inquiries, they hadn't heard of any relatives. The longer the time passed, the more she hoped he would remain with her. But then she felt guilty that she was wishing him to be deprived of his kin.

Suddenly there was a blast of early spring air, bringing with it damp early blossoms and grass, and male voices.

Alice rose and watched William, the center of a group of men, standing a head above them, listen to what one of them was saying. He was always like that: listening to people and then acting. Talking for the sake of it wasn't his thing, which was just as well, given her deafness. She got a thrill from watching how others looked up to him and how he controlled a situation with his presence alone.

She hadn't seen him alone in weeks, and she waited by the fire. His gaze rose to hers, and ignoring the others, he came over to her.

"My lady," he said, lifting her hand to his lips.

"William," she breathed, remembering the magic his lips had wrought on her own. "It is good to have you home."

"It'll be a brief visit. But I wished to come, for I bring news."

She brought her hand to her chest, glancing at Charles, who lay fast asleep, oblivious to the noise of the men around him.

William followed her gaze. "Charles's mother was making her way to Scotland to seek out a distant cousin who'd offered her shelter. The cousin is more than happy that the child is adopted by us."

Alice closed her eyes. She'd been dreading this moment, fearing the worst. But it was not the worst news, it was the best. "I can hardly believe it."

"All will be well for our family, Alice. You, me, the babe. You must believe it. There is nothing now that can tear us apart. I will make sure any last remaining feelings of fear or distrust are swept away."

Could life truly be changing for her after so many years? Alice hardly dared believe it. But, as she pressed her cheek to his chest and felt his arms around her, she believed him. For what could happen to them now?

CHAPTER 13

Alice paused by the church door. There it was. She did not need to read it, she'd read it often enough already to understand the words. But she couldn't get enough of the wedding notice—Sir William de Vere and Lady Alice de Courcy to be wed. She rarely continued to read the remainder of the notice, asking that if anyone knew any reasons why the two should not marry, they should come forward with that reason. Alice had no qualms on that front. They'd known each other so long and was certain there were no skeletons in either of their cupboards. No, she read the notice because it made real a future which she'd given up hoping for.

As she continued along the lane, back to the castle, it was as if the countryside reflected her revived spirits. Everywhere burst with spring beauty such as Alice could never remember.

Her new sisters smiled when she exclaimed at the opening blooms, at the birdsong which seemed to grow louder and sweeter with each passing day. Like the flowers, she felt as if she too, were opening her petals to the warm sunshine, leaving behind the dark and cold of winter.

There was only one thing which blotted her happiness and that was William's frequent absences, ensuring his lands were defended against the threat of invasion, a threat which Savari downplayed. Better than anyone, Savari knew the politics around the threat, and doubted it would eventuate.

But when William returned to the castle, late at night, exhausted from his work of raising money to arm his men and organize the defense of the long Norfolk coastline, he spent his time with Alice and Charles. No one questioned them as they spent time alone in the solar where Alice came to see a different side of William. One that was tender and patient, happy to show her what love could mean physically, but only going as far as she wanted. And she never had to tell him what she wanted or didn't want. In the same way he tended his land, he tended her—with patience and gentleness, coaxing out of her the girl he once knew.

And slowly, Alice's attitude to her wedding night was changing. She no longer looked upon it with dread, but more with anticipation.

Shortly after Alice arrived in the Hall, the door burst open, and Katherine entered, looking unusually harried.

"Has William returned?" Katherine asked.

"No, and where have you been?" asked Lora, who was helping mind baby Charles while Alice finalized the last-minute wedding arrangements.

Katherine unclasped her cloak and hung it up with an exasperated sigh. "I've been to Yarmouth, arguing with the captain. He really is…" Katherine hesitated, and Lora and Celestria turned and gave her their full attention. Katherine never hesitated. She blushed as they stared at her. "What?"

"You didn't finish your sentence," said Lora, jiggling

Charles on her hip as he began to fuss. "You always finish your sentences."

"It's what's so irritating about you," said Celestria.

Katherine shook her head. "How can finishing sentences be irritating?"

"Because you're always so certain, so dependable," said Celestria shrewdly. "I can't imagine what it's like to be so perfect."

Lora nodded in agreement, but Katherine busied herself with a pot the cook had brought in, tasting it and returning it to the kitchen with her approval. Alice noticed she kept her head down longer than usual, and the flush that filled her cheeks couldn't alone be put down to the heat from the fire. Alice didn't know what was going on in Katherine's world but had a suspicion that her increasingly frequent visits to Yarmouth were causing Katherine some kind of consternation. She decided to save her blushes.

"William sent me word that he's been held up in Norwich. He wanted to finish his business there before the wedding tomorrow."

"Good," said Katherine decisively, looking up, face composed once more. "I'll need his help with the problems with the boats. It seems the King has requisitioned everything to fight this phantom invasion. So my choices are limited."

Celestria raised an eyebrow. "To the mysterious captain."

Katherine resolutely ignored her. "Anyway, Alice, how is the dress?"

"Finished," Alice said, holding up the dress she'd been working on earlier, adding some fine gold thread around the throat.

Lora rose and felt the cloth between her fingers. "Even I love it, and I hate fancy dresses."

"That's because it's not fancy," said Celestria. "It's dignified, beautiful, understated, exactly like Alice." Alice blushed. She never used to blush, but now the walls around her were falling, she found her response to people was becoming more instant, less guarded. And, it appeared, there was little she could do about it. She wasn't even sure she wanted to anymore.

Alice brushed down the dress. "It's finer than anything I've ever worn."

"Blue for purity." Celestria winked. "And you, a mother."

Alice bit her lip and shook out the dress, hiding her expression from the others. Celestria didn't know what had happened to her, none of them did. Only William. Recovering herself, she shrugged and half-turned to them. "It's a little unusual, but I didn't want to let William down."

Katherine put her arm around her and pulled her close in a brief, comforting embrace. "William will love you in it."

Alice hoped so. She'd soon find out.

IT SEEMED there was to be no letting up of the sunshine that spring. And the day of their wedding dawned promising warmth and sunshine.

Alice and William led the small procession of family, friends, and villagers to the church. There was no one from her family's side. She'd heard nothing from her mother, but everyone else was there, apart from Savari.

"Where is he?" asked William. He looked out across the newly sprouted, green-dusted fields, toward where the road petered out into a haze. "He said he'd be here."

Alice shrugged. "He must have got held up. He wouldn't miss your wedding for no reason."

"Aye." He smiled at her. "You're right. And the only person I need is here." He squeezed her hand. She leaned her head against his arm in response. After so many years of having space between them, she couldn't get used to being able to touch him. She laughed as she had a vision of never allowing him to leave her again, clinging to him as the barnacles did to the boats.

He gave a grunt of laughter. "I love your laugh, it makes me laugh, even though I know not what it is which you find so funny."

They stopped at the church. "Mayhap that I can hardly believe my luck, can hardly believe this is happening," she said quietly.

"I can," he said. "It was always going to happen."

She shook her head in disbelief at William's certainty. She couldn't understand it, but she loved it and felt reassured by it. He moved as if to kiss her, but she smiled and retreated it. "Not until we're married, Sir William," she teased.

They entered the elaborate porch off the church, in front of the large oak doors, to be met by the priest. There were flowers everywhere, all along the ledges, and hanging from the ceiling as well. The porch, added by William's grandparents as a fitting place to exchange their wedding vows, was always a place of beauty with its vaulted ceiling and fine carvings, but now it was transformed into a spring arbor, complete with festoons of ribbons and greenery.

She turned and smiled at the culprits—Katherine, Celestria, and Lora, who grinned back—before taking her place to the left of William, facing the priest who stood in front of the door. Behind them, family and villagers finally hushed after the priest called for quiet. He cleared his throat and began the ceremony.

The priest, who Alice knew as a friendly, bumbling man who liked nothing better than to find a quiet corner of the castle Hall and consume copious amounts of wine, had been transformed into someone who was acutely aware of the gravitas of the ceremony.

"Does anyone know," he bellowed out to the congregation who gathered behind them, "of any reason why this couple should not be married?" His serious gaze swept across the people, and a deathly hush fell upon them, his question quieting the most eager gossiper. Alice suddenly felt a wave of nausea. What if someone did say something? Made something up, even? What if there was something in William's past he hadn't told her about?

William firmed his grip on her hand, sensing her tremble, and shot her a reassuring glance.

"And you, Sir William, and you, Lady Alice, do you know of any reason prohibiting your marriage?"

They both murmured their negative responses. The priest cleared his throat and resumed.

"Sir William, wilt thou have this woman to thy wedded wife, wilt thou love her, and honor her, keep her and guard her, in health and in sickness, as a husband should a wife, and forsaking all others on account of her, keep thee only unto her, so long as ye both shall live?"

"I will," said William in a loud, assertive voice, which prompted approving murmurs from the congregation.

"And wilt thou, Lady Alice, have this man to thy wedded husband, wilt thou love him, and honor him, keep him and guard him, in health and in sickness, as a wife should a husband, and forsaking all others on account of him, keep thee only unto him, so long as ye both shall live?"

"I will," said Alice firmly.

Savari was to have taken the role of her father, but as he still hadn't turned up, Sir Harry stepped forward and gave Alice away.

As William said his vows, his eyes fixed on her, Alice focused on trying to hold back the tears which threatened. It was only when he'd finished, and it was her turn, that she brushed her cheeks free of the tears. She cleared her throat and said the words back to him, their gaze never breaking, their hands entwined together.

"I, Alice take thee, William, to my wedded husband, to have and to hold from this day forward, for better, for worse, for richer, for poorer, in sickness, and in health, till death do us part, if the holy church will ordain it. And thereto I plight thee my troth."

She was barely aware of the priest blessing the rings which Sir Harry had handed to him. William brushed more tears from her cheeks with a smile. But the tears only flowed more strongly when she saw that the ring he slipped on her finger was his mother's, who'd died the year before. It was the final act that sealed the ceremony.

After the brief ceremony, they entered the church for the blessing and nuptial mass. As husband and wife, they knelt before the altar. They were married. *They were married,* she repeated to herself, barely aware of the priest's words, only of William's hand holding hers tightly. It seemed he also didn't want to let her go. And, after weeks of gentle wooing, she didn't want him to. She was looking forward to their wedding night.

As the afternoon rolled into evening and the feasting and festivities continued into the night, the one blot on the day was the absence of Savari. No word had been received from him, and Alice could tell that William was concerned. He'd sent Warin to Norwich to discover what had happened. His squire wasn't best pleased to miss out on the wedding feast but understood William's concerns. But even he hadn't yet returned.

"Savari can take care of himself, you know that, William," said Alice.

"Aye," said William, swirling his red wine around the goblet. "I do. But I also know something important is afoot, as he'd not miss his brother's wedding for no reason."

It was also what Alice was thinking, but she wanted to reassure William, not increase his worries. "Most likely it's a reason to do with the King that's preventing him from being here. And the King believes everything to do with him to be of the greatest import."

"Aye, you're probably right, wife."

The last word he uttered brought a strange fizzing to her gut and lower. "Wife," she repeated as he sat closer to her. "I like the sound of that on your lips."

He lifted her chin with his finger, forcing her embarrassed gaze higher. "I would have more on my lips than a word. I'd have you."

The fizzing intensified, and her heart began to beat a rapid tattoo. She swallowed, and his eyes darkened in response.

"It is late," she said. "Mayhap, it is time to retire?"

A wide grin spread over his face. "Aye, I reckon it's time."

He rose and offered his hand to her. Whoops and roars of satisfaction swept around the merry crowd as William escorted Alice to the stairway. As people began to follow, she did what she knew she had to do. As William sheltered her from prying eyes, she slipped a garter from her leg and tossed it to the crowd. Better that than being accompanied to the bridal chamber by hordes of friends, relatives, and guests.

Blushing, Alice refused the many offers to help her out of her wedding clothes. Even if *her* refusals had been ignored, no one dared to ignore William's firm refusal. With a final farewell, he closed the door to the stairs, and the roar became muffled by the thick walls, as he led her up the stairs to their bedchamber.

Alice entered the bedchamber and walked across to the bed. Her heart was thumping, and she felt breathless as she fingered the flowers which decorated the bed.

"Your sisters must have plucked every bloom in the garden."

"It is their way of showing you how much they welcome you into their lives."

"They have been very kind."

"Relieved, I think, to know that their brother will be alone no longer."

She turned to find he hadn't moved. He stood in front of the oak door, his hands still behind him where he'd pushed the door closed.

"But you were never alone. You were always surrounded by your family, by your friends, your people. Always." The thought that he'd felt alone had never crossed her mind.

"Aye," he said, pushing himself from the door and stepping to the bed, where he picked up one bloom after another. "I'm always surrounded by people, but I always felt alone. My thoughts were with you, Alice. You must know that. Since we were children, my world has centered around you."

She passed him a flower to add to his growing bouquet. "I'd never imagined you felt alone. You always seemed…" she trailed off.

"Busy was what I was. It was my answer to my loneliness." He handed her the bouquet, and she sniffed it, closing her eyes as she let the smell and feelings fill her. He touched her hair, and she opened her eyes. "I thought I'd feel surprised, unable to believe my luck on this night. But all I feel is relief."

Tears pricked her eyes, but she blinked them away. She wanted to see him clearly. She wanted to absorb every minute thing about him.

"William," she said, her voice sounding hoarse, strained. She reached out her hand, wondering as to his hesitation. "Please, come. Place your hands on me and help me disrobe."

He shook his head and for one long, awful moment, Alice

wondered if he'd had a change of heart. If, after such a long time of wanting her, he didn't want her anymore.

She gave a strangled sob. "Why won't you come?"

He shook his head, and huffed out a deep breath. "Because I am afeared you will not welcome my touch."

She gave a relieved smile. "Believe me, I do." She reached out further to him. "Please come to me."

"Are you sure?" he asked. "I wondered..."

"If," she helped out, "after what happened, I wouldn't want to consummate our marriage?"

He nodded.

"I didn't. And that is the truth. But these past weeks together, you have taught me that what happened to me is a thing apart from what happens between us. When you touch me, I'm not repelled—"

He grinned. "*That*, my love, is a start."

She laughed and shook her head. "Let me finish. No, when you touch me, all I can think about is about how much more I want you to touch me. How I want you to touch not only my hand, or my face, but my arm, my shoulder, my neck, and..." She hesitated but blushed and was unable to name the parts of her she wished him to touch so intimately. "And more," she finished with a smile.

"More?" he said. "I like the sound of that." But still he didn't move.

"I want you, William, with all my heart and body, I want you. Now!" She added emphasis to the last word, anxious that he understand her.

He nodded slowly. "Your command, my lady, is my wish."

And then he came to her.

CHAPTER 14

He didn't need any further persuasion or commanding. He bridged the distance between them with two steps and took the bouquet from her and tossed it to one side, the blooms scattering across the rush floor, already woven with fragrant flower heads.

He took her hands and pressed them against his lips. His eyes were closed, and she brushed her hand against his brow, pushing away the heavy lock of dark hair which lay against his tanned forehead.

When he felt her touch, he looked up at her with his dark, dark eyes which she could read like a book. She saw her own desire reflected there.

He groaned and pulled her toward him. He placed his hands either side of her face and gently tilted her head up to meet his gaze. "Do you know what this means?"

She nodded. "Aye, of course I do. I want you to love me like a husband loves his wife." Her voice quavered a little as she spoke the last words, and she swallowed. His eyes flickered down to the movement of her throat, which betrayed her underlying nerves. She knew what she wanted. She knew it in her head, but her body was hesitant.

"You are afraid," he said. "You mustn't be. If this is something you truly wish, then I will take it slowly, step by step, so that you always know what I intend, and you will always wish for me to continue. That, I promise."

She inhaled a deep breath, loving the masculine smell of him still tinged with the scent of fresh air and grass which lingered on his clothes.

He smiled, and she raised her finger, and tentatively drew it along his bottom lip. Something she'd always longed to do. It felt softer than it looked, and she drew confidence in the sharp intake of breath that her action initiated. Without a thought, she raised herself on tiptoe and pressed her lips to his.

It was as if she'd cast a spell upon him, and he didn't move, didn't breathe even. She pulled away with a gasp and looked at him. He shook his head and thrust his fingers into her hair, loosening it from its bindings. She could feel tension in his fingers as they pressed against her head. He let out a shuddering breath, and then his lips were upon hers once more, except this time, there was no hesitation.

His lips held hers in thrall as they pressed against them, moving over hers with sensuous control, which sent lightning strikes of desire sparking through her. Whatever part of her they touched, deep inside of her, they brought to life, set to fire. But it wasn't a fire which consumed, it was a fire that renewed. It was all the confirmation she needed that she'd set her past well and truly behind her. She was his now, truly and completely, and she wanted nothing more. The heat spread through her limbs, melting them as her heart and mind grew more fiery and desirous. His arms proved strong and supportive, as her legs became unsteady.

He was holding her now, his body pressed against hers,

and she felt his arousal against her belly. Her heart leaped into a sharp staccato of desire as she imagined what he was about to do, and she felt his quickened breath against her mouth. He pulled away.

"Alice, oh, Alice," he exhaled, shaking his head in wonderment. "I'd imagined this moment for so long." His eyes ranged over her as he brushed her hair off her face.

"Me also." His grin widened, but she didn't smile back. "And now it is here, and I would have you kiss me again."

He didn't need asking twice, and his mouth was over hers immediately, only this time, the sensations were heightened as his tongue slid between her lips as if testing to see if they'd open. She opened her mouth, and a moan escaped as his tongue found entry and slid and played with the tip of her tongue. A fierce lick of flame coiled inside her, and she knew that she wanted him to enter, not only her mouth but also another part of her. She knew she'd give William anything he asked.

She pushed herself against him harder, wanting to feel the full length of his muscled body against hers. What she found wasn't what she'd expected. His cock was hard and pressed into her stomach, seemingly much too large to enter her body. She withdrew in shock.

But he wouldn't allow her to draw back fully. His hands were on her shoulders, holding her still. "Do not be frightened, my love. I promise I will be gentle."

She nodded. It wasn't as if she were still a maid. That had been taken from her, and she knew the pain wouldn't be so great as it had been then. She nodded again. "I'll try not to be, but…"

He lifted her chin. "All you have to do is enjoy my touch, to allow yourself to surrender to the demands of your body."

"But I do not understand my body's demands."

"You shall," he said.

He undid the brooch at her neck and pulled her dress from her shoulders. She felt the rush of cool air hit her neck before his lips descended, bringing a bloom of heat wherever his lips touched her skin. They left a trail of raised goose-bumps as he descended lower to the top of her breasts, which she now realized were heaving as if she were out of breath. She pulled at the neck and then twirled around.

"Undo the laces, please William."

It took several attempts, but he did as she asked, and her gown pooled to the floor. She stepped out of it. She was now standing only in her chemise, shivering slightly. William gripped her waist before sweeping his thumbs beneath her breasts. And then higher as they brushed the tightening nubs of her nipples. Her breathing was coming even faster now, and she was aware of a needy throbbing between her legs.

She put her arms around him and lifted her mouth to be kissed once more. She wanted nothing more than his lips and tongue upon her, relishing the sense of invasion of his body into hers. His mouth covered hers as she ground her body, all hesitation forgotten, against his. She no longer felt fearful of his hard cock, but welcomed its pressure against the soft flesh of her belly and lower, where the throbbing was centered and where his hardness rubbed, sending shivers of arousal rippling through her body.

His hands roved over her now, exploring her body through the thin stuff of her shift. He placed his hands over her bottom, caressing its shape before cupping it and lifting her tighter against him.

He laid her gently on the bed, one leg between her legs as he knelt over her. She felt wanton as he looked at her, her hair fanned over the coverlet, her shift hitched up to her thighs.

"You are so beautiful," he murmured before kissing her. He lay over her, propping his weight on one arm, his leg between hers. She gasped at the pressure of his thigh against the apex of her legs—a sensitive place, which was proving needy and demanding.

She writhed lightly against him, all thought of decorum gone, all signs of fear vanished. All she wanted was for the spellbinding sensation which his body exerted upon hers to intensify. She did not know how that could be, nor did she know what would happen as it increased, but she only knew, without a doubt, that she needed more.

As if sensing her heightened need, he swept up her chemise until it lay bunched around her waist. She blushed and stilled, the cool air against her most private parts making her feel more exposed than she'd ever been. But then those clever lips fell upon her, and all fears were swept away.

His breath was hot upon her stomach, but not as hot as his mouth, and then his tongue. She closed her eyes, and her breath hitched as his tongue trailed down her belly and found its target. She jumped. "Holy Mary," she uttered. "Surely that"—again her breath hitched—"isn't God's work."

He looked up with a grin. "All good things are God's work, my love." He descended once more and Alice had no more thought of God or the Devil, or good or evil, only what her body wanted. And her body demanded more of the pleasure which washed over her in heat-prickling waves, making her fingertips tingle, and her breathing quicken, as if she were running for something, but not quite reaching it. And then she was there, teetering on the edge of something unknowable. With one more suckle and sweep of his tongue, Alice found what was on the other side of such pleasure—waves and waves rolling over and through her of blissful release. Her body shook with the strength of it. And she knew that all would be well.

When she opened her eyes, William was standing over her, pulling off his clothes. The light from the fire's flames flickered over his body, strong and brown from a lifetime of being outside. His muscles were beautiful—they gleamed as if burnished. She wanted to cup their curves and run her fingers over every part of him. He was so strong, and she felt so slight. She wanted to surrender to him in a way she'd never thought possible. The notion sent another wave of desire pulsing through her.

He stepped out of his breeches, his hard cock thrusting forward, every inch of it showing his intention. She'd thought she'd be frozen with fear at this moment but, instead, she was intensely curious—released by the pleasure he'd given her. She reached out to him.

"Alice," he said.

"I want to touch it, to know it." She touched his cock, and it twitched. With one finger, she tentatively touched the soft exposed skin at its end. He drew in a sharp breath and closed his eyes. She grew braver, fascinated by the power she had over him now. She swept her fingers over his cock, down to the base where she cupped the soft sack. "I would know everything about you, William. Everything," she said, surprised at the huskiness of her voice.

"And me, you. Now," he said, "lie back."

She immediately did as she was told. During the day, she would not be so acquiescent, but now, she yearned to be. She lay back on the bed, acutely aware of the softness of the fur against her bare skin. He knelt over her and kissed her. Then he slowly lowered himself, taking his weight on his hands while holding her where he needed her to be, and where she wanted to be.

She felt his cock nudge at the apex between her legs. She opened her legs wider to allow him in, and it slid in easily at first.

"Oh," he groaned. "You are so wet." He pushed further and kissed her again, and the slight tension she'd suddenly felt dissolved under the magic his lips wrought. And when he lifted his mouth from her, she felt him ease himself inside a little further still. He paused then and licked his fingers, and brought his hand between their two bodies. Alice was puzzled, then he found her mound and ran his wet fingers around it. She gasped both at the intimacy and burst of desire which he ignited, as his fingers continued to circle and stimulate her. Her breathing was coming faster now, and she gripped his shoulders. He pulled his fingers away and slid all the way inside her.

For a moment, he looked at her, his cock firmly inside her, at her center, holding her in place, claiming her for his own. And then he shifted, and she felt a delicious feeling inside of her, which made her call out.

"What is it? Do you wish me to stop?" His eyes showed concern.

"No! I want more!" She shifted against him, wriggling to move him deeper inside of her, to find that place which he'd just touched, which gave her such pleasure. "I want this like nothing else." He laughed a deep guttural laugh which she felt through her body. And then he pulled out of her. "No!"

But she need not have worried, for it was only briefly. For he immediately pushed deep inside of her, and she gripped the fur coverlets as a profusion of sensations filled her. Then he pulled out and pushed inside her again. Each time he did this, the tension inside her coiled and heightened.

He was careful at first but, as he realized she felt no pain and no longer any fear, he quickened his movements. She grew confident and pushed against him, making him forget his caution, making him go faster until suddenly her world stopped, and a blaze of light filled her head and body. She cried out his name at the same time he cried out hers, and then she felt him shudder and tighten and push inside her with short urgent thrusts.

As he withdrew, he put his arms around her, and together they rolled onto their sides. She felt his seed leak from between her legs, mixed with her own juices. She was bound to him now as she'd never been before. Not with the wedding, not with their adoption of Charles. But with this lovemaking, which had caught them in its thrall and had tethered them together forever. She pressed herself against him and kissed him without softness, wanting to show him the fierceness of her love, and he returned the kiss with equal hunger.

Soon she felt him harden against her, as she'd wanted, and she opened her legs to receive him. She snapped her eyes closed as the sensations filled her once more. Her body was attuned now to his, and she was aware of his every movement. This time William held nothing back. As her fingertips bit into his arms, he thrust inside her, guided by her needs, which turned out to be great. She tasted his neck with her tongue and her teeth, and he grunted as he registered each nip and suckle, and drove harder into her, pushing her farther along the soft furs with each thrust.

It was not over so quickly this time. The ecstasy held, and didn't explode but was sustained by each other's movements as they both savored not only the physical, but the connection of mind and soul. When the climax came, it arrived with a cry from Alice and a fierce pumping of William's seed into her. It was a claiming—that much she knew, and that much she wanted.

They fell into each other's arms, a tangle of slick legs and bodies held close. Slowly, oh so slowly, Alice's mind drifted away on a rolling wave of complete and utter satiation that felt as if it would travel toward eternity, leaving her past well and truly behind her.

. . .

By the time the morning came, William knew that Alice would be sore, but it still seemed she wanted him. And he was in no mood to deny her.

The sky was lightening, and they could hear the sounds of day breaking, people moving, and a lone horse approaching at a gallop. No doubt a messenger. But even that didn't break his focus.

He held her close, their mouths only a breath apart, as he slipped inside her, and his heart swelled as she gasped with pleasure and closed her eyes. He kissed both eyelids, marveling that at last, he had the intimacy he desired with her, and at how open she'd been to his lovemaking. It seemed he'd underestimated how sensual Alice was behind those barriers which had shielded her real self for so long.

Now, as she gripped his shoulders and he pushed into her, hitching her breath higher with each thrust, he thought he hardly knew where his flesh began, and hers ended. They were all one, and would always be.

Suddenly there was a thunderous knocking on the door of their bedchamber.

"Go away," bellowed William, before Alice gasped as she reached her climax, her body tell-tale limp as he finished coming inside of her.

The footsteps retreated, and he turned his attention back to Alice. He'd thought possessing her would be enough. But now he'd had a taste of what it was like to make love to a woman such as Alice, he knew he'd never get enough.

He stroked her nipple with his thumb and then kissed her skin where his thumb had been. He loved how sensitive she was. How she twitched slightly and gasped as his mouth covered her breast, and he suckled long and hard, drawing her nipple into his mouth, laving it with his tongue. He was hard and ready to take her again when there was another knock at the door. This time it was more urgent.

"William!" the voice commanded. William's head snapped around to the door. It was Savari. He'd arrived at last.

William rolled off Alice even though her hand reached out to keep him in place. His gaze swept her naked body, and he almost forgot the voice, but it came again louder this time.

"William! I have pressing news."

William stroked Alice's skin and watched her stomach flicker under his ministrations. "It'll have to wait. I have my own pressing concerns." He eased himself over Alice once more.

"None such as this! You must come immediately. This won't wait."

William rolled off Alice and took a deep breath as he tried to think of something which would enable him to greet Savari without his cock protruding from beneath his robe. He swore under his breath again. "I'm coming." He rose and pulled on his shirt and breeches. At the door, he looked back at Alice, who drew the covers over herself. He took another breath and opened the door.

Savari stood before him, leaning on one hand on the door jamb. His face was grim, and his clothes travel-stained. "I've come from Norwich. I had to wait until I knew for sure."

"Knew what? What could be so important that you would miss my wedding?"

"I had to await confirmation that the courts had upheld the accusation."

"What accusation? You talk in riddles."

"William. Come away, I would have this conversation in your chamber, not in the corridor."

Suddenly Alice appeared behind William, pulling on her cloak over her robe. William drew her close, enveloping her in his arms protectively.

"We are married now, Savari," said Alice. "What affects

my husband affects me. There will be no more secrets between us."

William looked at his beloved wife and wondered if his life could ever be more perfect. His answer was immediately forthcoming.

"Have it your way. William, the sergeant is on his way here. I've beaten him by only an hour at most. They are coming to arrest you for the murder of Ralph de Gant."

CHAPTER 15

William swore as the perfection of his night dissolved into chaos. He dropped his arm from Alice, whose pallor betrayed her shock.

"What happened?" he asked Savari as he finished dressing.

"Adam de Gant is what happened." Savari followed him into the room, only giving the rumpled bed sheets a cursory glance before focusing on William. "He turned up at the Norwich Courts two days ago with…" He paused. "Allegations."

"Allegations which are true," murmured William.

"You had no choice!" said Alice. William turned to look at her and found, not his beautiful reserved wife, but a stunning warrior. Her eyes flashed as she pulled her robe tighter around her. She came to him and gripped both his arms. "You had no choice," she said more quietly but with equal urgency.

"We always have a choice. And I made mine and will live with the consequences."

Alice's eyes widened, and she turned from William, never taking her hands from him and fixed Savari with a fierce gaze. "All William did was to protect me. If William hadn't killed him, he'd have killed William and me eventually. This charge cannot stand."

Savari opened the door. "It can and it will. We need to talk and prepare."

They walked downstairs into the Hall, which still bore the evidence of the previous night's wedding festivities. Servants had been roused and were building up the fires to take the edge off the spring morning, which had had no chance to warm.

Savari went to the fire, his back to William and Alice, who exchanged anxious glances.

It was only when the servants had withdrawn that Savari turned to them. William didn't think he'd ever seen Savari's handsome face so bleak and exhausted.

"You should go, Alice. The maid will be drawing you a bath. There is no need for you to hear any of this."

But she remained staunchly by his side. "We are one, now, William. What concerns you concerns me." She turned to Savari with a self-possession William could only admire. "You may speak freely in front of me. After all, what has happened is because of me, and I take full responsibility."

William had always known his Alice was brave, but seeing her stand so strongly beside him, made him choke up. He shrugged and turned back to Savari. "Tell us everything."

Savari recounted how Adam de Gant had appeared out of nowhere demanding justice, and how Savari had been unable to do anything other than watch and wait as the sergeant on duty had weighed the evidence and issued a writ for William's arrest. It had meant missing their wedding and had only given him the slimmest head start in reaching William before the bailiffs and sergeant did.

"They're on their way to arrest you, William. And there is no persuading them otherwise."

"There is nothing you can say to stop them, brother. There is no way out," said William pacing the floor. "I killed a man, and there was a witness."

"A witness who is the dead man's son. It's his word against yours."

"You forget there is evidence that we were the only people present. The servants know that, others know that. If I didn't kill him, then who? His son?" William shook his head. "No. There is no way out of this."

"Yes, there is," said Alice. Her voice was so quiet that William didn't hear it at first. "Yes, there is," she said more firmly. Savari snapped his head to look at her.

"How so?" he asked.

"Alice," said William, in a warning tone.

She ignored him. "Adam de Gant might be able to prove it was William who killed him, but if you put me on the stand, I can attest to it being in self-defense."

"I will not have it!" thundered William. "Alice is too delicate to be put on the stand. It would be demeaning."

"Nonsense, William." William frowned and looked at Alice with new eyes. It seemed the night of lovemaking had changed her, brought out a strength in her he'd only sensed before. "I am not so delicate that I cannot provide a reason for my husband to kill the man who tried to force me into marriage!"

Savari nodded before turning to William. "It seems you have a warrior for a wife, William!" He rose. "It will work."

"I don't want Alice publicly humiliated," William growled, knowing he was fighting a losing battle.

"Nor do I," said Savari. "But unless you wish to lose your life, it would appear we have to." Outside could be heard the clatter of horses' hooves and shouts from the de Vere guards, which ended abruptly. Inside, all was icy calm. Savari rubbed his bottom lip with his finger, his eyes narrowed in thought.

Then he nodded. "It could work, William. If Alice is prepared to stand up in court and describe how she was taken by force—"

"It would be their word against ours. Yet again."

"But there will be more than one man who can confirm Alice's version of events. And if she's believed, then your plea will be self-defense, and the case will be transferred to the King's justice for pardon. And I can then pave the way for acquittal on the grounds Alice describes."

Suddenly, the door burst open, and the court bailiffs rushed over to William and grabbed his arms. He looked at Alice, his eyes narrowed with command. "No," was the last word he spoke as he was escorted from his chamber, his Hall, and lastly from his castle.

Alice rushed after him, stumbling over the uneven ground of the bailey yard, holding onto the gatehouse pillar as she watched the men gallop off with William's arms firmly tied behind him.

In desperation, she turned to Savari. After everything they'd thought and hoped for during the night, this was to be it? No, it couldn't be; it wouldn't be.

"We must *do* something. We cannot simply let him leave like this!"

"We can do little else. If you have the courage to do as you say, then we may win yet."

As Alice watched the dust settle behind William and his gaolers, she knew she had to find the courage, because he'd saved her from a life of no feeling, and it was her turn to save him.

THE WEEKS PASSED in a frenzy of heightened emotions at Wanham and heated discussions between Alice, Savari, and the lawyers. If it hadn't been for Katherine's steadiness of purpose, Alice thought she wouldn't have coped. But her support gave Alice strength, and she needed every ounce of it now, as she stood in the courtroom, waiting for William to appear from the gaol below.

Alice's mouth dried as William walked up the stairs at the back of the room. The weeks had wrought their changes on him. His hair was longer, his body leaner, and his eyes—Alice's heart nearly stopped, and she brought her hands to her breast—his eyes were savage and angry as they roved the courtroom, hungry for something. He soon found his target. Once his gaze was locked on her, his eyes lost their anger, but the heat flared, and Alice knew she'd have a battle on her hands if she were to stick to the defense that she and Savari had agreed upon.

The noise of the people in the courtroom suddenly burst upon her senses with a roar as William's supporters demonstrated loudly against his incarceration.

A gavel banged onto the wooden desk. "Silence! By order of the Judge of this esteemed court, I bid you all be silent, damn you!" the bailiff added irritably.

William swept a quietening glance around the chamber, and his people fell quiet.

"All rise for the Judge!" instructed the court official. The Judge entered and looked around with a supercilious air.

"So, Sir William," said the Judge, making himself comfortable. "It is charged that you did, in cold blood, murder Sir Ralph de Gant. What say you?"

"I did not kill him in cold blood—"

"What say you to the charge!" bellowed the court official.

"Not guilty."

Alice let out a long-held breath. She'd been worried that he'd plead 'guilty', but sense—either his or Savari's—had prevailed.

The court sat back with shufflings and mutterings, to settle themselves for the duration.

As witnesses for the prosecution were called forward and gave their version of events, Alice's concern grew. Some lied, some gave the truth, but their statements all backed up Adam de Gant's allegations—that William killed Adam's father in cold blood.

Whenever Savari, as William's lawyer, tried to intervene, his arguments were shot down. Matters were no better when it came to the turn of the defense. The Judge was determined to allow a picture to be painted of William as an opportunist, wanting Alice, and determined to kill for her.

"And you, the accused, for some unknown reason"—the Judge rolled his eyes before taking a sip of wine—"decided to visit the castle." He sat back. "I wonder why? Designs of your own, mayhap?"

Before William could speak, Savari stepped forward. "My Lord, you must understand, William and Lady Alice are friends of old."

"I did not ask for your interpretation of events, sir!" The Judge glared at William. "No. I've heard enough." The court official rose, slamming his stick against the wooden floor. "Sir William de Vere, you stand accused of murdering Ralph de Gant. What say you?"

"It is true. I killed him."

There was a gasp in the room and a cry from Alice, but William didn't look at her.

"Your honor," said Adam de Gant to the Judge. "I would not forgo the pleasure of revenge. I would accept a trial by ordeal. A fight to the death between us."

The boy had nowhere near William's strength, being not yet fully grown. For all the hatred which burned in his eyes for William, Alice knew that William's superior strength would mean he'd easily win the battle. William turned to the

Judge. "I will not fight him. Sentence me and be done with it."

"No!" Alice called out, approaching the bench as close as she could. The crowd parted a little, and she pressed forward again, shaking her head, her face white but her voice steady. "No! This must not be. It is all because of me."

"Be done with it," said William, not looking at Alice, but staring directly at the Judge. But the Judge held up his hand.

"I will listen to what the lady has to say before I pass sentence. My lady?" He nodded at her. "Please, take the stand and speak."

A hush descended on the room. Even the gossips were quiet, straining to peer at Alice above the heads of others. "What did she say?" one asked. "She's said nothing yet, you fool. Be quiet."

William's face was white as he looked across at her. "Alice," he pleaded under his breath.

She shook her head, conjuring up all the strength she usually kept hidden from the world, before turning to the Judge. "I was taken by force to Ralph de Gant, where he held me against my will. William found out and came to rescue me. Ralph de Gant intended to force me into marriage."

There was a gasp of outrage across the court.

"This is beside the point, Your Honor." Adam de Gant shook his head and looked at William. "Sir William murdered my father. And that is all there is to the matter!"

"Quiet!" The Judge glared around the courtroom. "Go on," he said to Alice, once order reigned once more.

"He held me captive in his castle in Lincolnshire. There he intended to do what he wished with me. Wed or otherwise."

The murmurings grew—some sympathetic, some horrified, some excited—but everyone hanging on her every word.

The Judge frowned and steepled his fingers and rubbed his lips. He grunted and cleared his throat. "These are serious allegations, Lady Alice."

"They are, Your Honor. But they are not charges, they are the truth. Sir William, the accused, has been my friend since childhood. When I was taken by force to Lincolnshire, William came to rescue me, knowing full well what would lie in store for me otherwise."

"He is a good knight!" came a shout from the crowds. Others picked up the call, and soon the place was in chaos.

The court bailiff called for order, slamming the stick onto the floor. His clerks did the same.

"William killed Ralph de Gant in self-defense," continued Alice. "If he had not, William would now be dead. And he did this to rescue me from a marriage which was hateful to me."

"But it is only your word we have that you were held in Lincolnshire by force." He shrugged and turned to Adam de Gant. "What say you? Did it appear that this lady came to the castle of her own free will?"

Everyone looked at Adam.

Alice almost felt sorry for him. He had, after all, lost a father, and was about to lose his case. She caught his eye and saw something different to his father there, and knew she'd won.

He shook his head. "I cannot deny it." He spat the words out like they tasted poisonous to his lips.

"You were a party to this, sir?" asked the Judge.

He shook his head. "I knew nothing of the plan until she was brought to the castle. And then I saw what had happened. He held her against her will, and he intended to marry her by force. He wanted her lands."

The court was in an uproar, and Adam's accusations lay in tatters.

Above the noise, the Judge called for order. He rose from

the bench. "Given the new information, I declare that Sir William de Vere, Earl of Winterton, did as a good and courteous knight should, rescuing a defenseless noblewoman from a lawless marriage. The crime is excusable as he killed Ralph de Gant in defense of a lady. And for this, he must obtain a royal pardon." He nodded to William's guards, who hauled him off into the gaol below.

"Savari! Take care of her!" were William's last words. But his last look was to Alice.

"What's going on?" Alice asked Savari. She'd thought he would be released instantly.

She looked around. The people bayed for William's release, but the old ways were no longer sufficient. King John's father had brought in new ways of justice which overruled the old ways which were often tempered by the feeling of the community. No longer. The King was in charge, and everyone must know it.

They were being jostled, but Savari held onto her firmly and managed to get her through the crowds and outside. But she pulled away. "Savari! We must set him free!"

"We will. *I* will," he corrected himself.

Tears ran down her face, unstoppable now. She couldn't think straight. All she could see was William's back disappearing into the darkness of the gaol. He'd hate it down there. He loved the light and the earth. She squeezed her eyes shut tight at the dread which seized her at the thought of what he would be feeling.

Then she felt two strong hands over hers and a slight shake. She opened her eyes to see Savari's handsome face, his pale blue eyes cutting into hers. "You have to be strong, Alice. You must leave it to me."

"But I thought—"

"And you thought correct. You saved him from death by hanging. You had the verdict changed, and now he has a chance of escaping the hangman's noose. *You* did that. And there is nothing more you can do except return to Wanham and keep safe. Safe until the time William is free to return."

"But when will that be?"

Savari hesitated, his teeth grinding, and Alice knew that things weren't as simple as he'd described them.

He exhaled. "I know not. The King is away at present. And the Chief Justiciar is preoccupied. I believe he'll delegate the decision."

"Delegate?" Alice's mouth dried. "To whom?"

"To the Sheriff of Norfolk and Suffolk."

"Sir Bayard of Wrotham?" It was worse news than she anticipated.

"Aye, he was appointed thus on Ralph de Gant's recommendation. I will do whatever it takes," he said grimly, before dropping her hands and nodding to William's squire. "See Lady Alice safely home," he said.

"No, I must stay," said Alice. But Savari insisted, and William's squire pulled her out of the way.

"You *must* do as Sir Savari says," said Warin loudly, trying to be heard above the melee. "He knows what's best for Sir William now."

No, she thought, miserably, he doesn't. Only I can extricate William from the mess that was mine to begin with. She stumbled outside into the brilliant sunshine and twisted around, trying to catch sight of the gaol where she knew William languished. It was like a dark hole, a pit from which all sunlight had been extinguished. She gave another wail and was flung onto her horse. The squire jumped up behind her while other men joined them front and back, and they galloped away. Away from where William lay. Imprisoned. Because of her.

She didn't cry now. She felt stilled again, but not into ice, not into inertia anymore, but into strength. She'd do what she had to do and free William from the darkness into which she'd cast him, if it were the last thing she did.

She'd do anything to release William. Anything. Even if it meant seeing once more the one man whom she hated above everyone, the one man who had the power to free William.

CHAPTER 16

It wasn't hard to fool everyone, Alice discovered. She'd never done it before, had always been honest in her dealings. It had made people trust her, something they'd never do again when they discovered what she was about to do. Only Celestria looked suspicious. Alice wasn't surprised by that. Celestria was the only one of the sisters whose intelligence was matched by a recklessness and disregard for convention. Alice suspected Celestria would have done as Alice was doing, except without the subterfuge.

"Where did you say you were going?" asked Celestria.

Alice gave her one of her coolest looks, perfected over the years. "I don't believe I did." She continued with her stitchwork. Anything that would keep her fingers busy and give her mind the ability to range over her plans, searching for fishhooks, anything that might trip her up.

Celestria rose, dropped her book noisily on the table so that all the women looked up, and walked to Alice. She rolled back on her heels, lifted her chin, and clasped her hands firmly before her. "Then, pray, tell me."

"Celestria!" admonished Katherine. "It is none of your business. Alice can come and go as she wishes."

"Of course. I did not say she couldn't. I merely wondered what her destination was. What her purpose was."

"That, sister, is none of your business." Katherine turned to Alice. "Please, forgive Celestria. She is hasty. Mother and Father always indulged her too much."

Celestria snorted and turned away, her interest already waning. She waved her hand. "Mother and Father could not handle me. And nor can anyone. I am my own woman."

Lora rolled her eyes. "So you think."

Celestria glared at her. "So I know." She turned back to Alice. "Anyway, I'm sure whatever it is you're up to, it'll be for the good of my brother."

Alice contemplated whether to bring her sisters by marriage into her plans but thought better of it. It was simpler that way. Nothing could interfere with what she planned.

As Alice left Wanham Castle with only William's squire for company, she was determined. She wasn't going to her old home as her sisters-in-law imagined, she was going to Norwich. For on this day, she knew that the newly appointed Sheriff of Norfolk and Suffolk—Sir Bayard of Wrotham—was in residence. For just two days. But she'd only need one.

ALICE AND WARIN made it as far as the outskirts of Norwich without incident. There, they met one of Savari's men who had a message for Alice. She tore open the missive eagerly, scanning it with disappointment. Savari was doing his best, she knew. But, in this case, it wasn't enough to free William—some things only she could do.

She knew where to go. She'd been there often enough at Christmas and other times of family gatherings. She dismounted from her horse and looked up at the grand house on the old square which had once belonged to her grandparents. Summoning all her courage, she rapped on the front door.

She was granted immediate entrance. But only to see the seneschal.

"Lady Alice." The seneschal didn't smile but clicked his fingers for refreshment and seated her before the fire. "It is a cold and unfriendly day to be riding so far from home."

She gratefully took a sip of the wine, allowing its warmth to travel through her body and give her aid to say what she needed. "It is, sir. But I have good reason. I would see your master, my father's cousin"—she didn't think it would hurt to state her relationship with the hated man—"Sir Bayard at once."

The seneschal inclined his head in acknowledgment, but his expression didn't change. "I'm afraid that's not possible. His lordship is busy with business since his recent appointment."

She placed her cup onto the table with a reassuringly steady hand and fixed her iciest, most commanding gaze upon him. "And *I* am here on business." She paused, giving the seneschal a moment to digest this fact. "Business," she emphasized, "which he will be glad to know of."

The seneschal's eyes flickered narrowly as he digested her words. It all hung on her ability to get through to this man. She could speak, she could plead, but instead she did as instinct told her, she kept quiet and rested her gaze on him. It was he in the end who broke the connection. His eyes slid away, and she knew she had him.

His tongue flickered from between his lips, and Alice was reminded of a snake, an adder's tongue, tasting the air, sensing danger.

"I will inform his lordship you are here. I assume the business is about your husband, Sir William?"

"You assume correctly. I have additional information which I think his lordship will find most pertinent to the case."

"I hope so, for both our sakes."

Without a further word, he opened a black oak door and walked into the Hall. Alice could hear his lordship speaking with others as the door opened and closed.

She took a deep breath. The first hurdle was over. She would see the man who held William's life in his hands. And she would have to give the performance of her life.

The seneschal was back with her quicker than she'd anticipated. "His lordship will see you now. He can spare you only minutes. You must make your case swiftly."

She didn't need telling that. She brushed her hand down her gown and, summoning up all her courage, swept into the Hall, looking, she hoped, every inch a respectable woman of property. She came to a halt and bowed before him.

"Lady Alice." The sound of that so familiar voice sent shivers down her spine. But she dredged up all her strength from deep inside of her. She was no longer thirteen years of age. She was a woman, a woman who was loved, and a woman who gave love, a woman not to be browbeaten.

"Your lordship." She looked up into his gray eyes and, despite her intentions, felt the familiar repulsion gather in her gut.

"I did not expect to see you. Yet you came of your own accord."

"I did. I came to free William. Only you can do that."

"And why would I want to?"

"Because unless you do, the world will know what kind of man you are." Suddenly he looked less sure. She decided to press on while she had the advantage of surprise. "I suggest you dismiss your men."

There were mutterings from his clerks. Alice heard the words "impudence," and "slut", but ignored them all. She only had eyes for the monster before her. He opened his mouth to speak, and she raised a warning eyebrow. It seemed that he was aware of her every nuanced expression. He waved his men to leave.

Finally, the door clanged shut, and they were alone. Something she'd vowed she'd never be again with him.

"You would not dare," he finally said.

"Dare what? Tell the world that the great Sheriff of Norfolk and Suffolk is nothing more than an incestuous rapist? That he vilely abused both his cousin's daughter and wife while his own cousin…" She hesitated after she spat out the word, still unable to understand how this man could have done what he'd done to his own flesh and blood. She inhaled a calming breath. "While his own cousin," she repeated, "believed his family to be safe in his care."

"You would ruin yourself in the process." He rose and loomed over her, as he'd always done, hoping to intimidate her. "That, child, is why you will not say anything."

"You've miscalculated on three counts. One, I am no longer a child. Two, you don't intimidate me. And three, I have no care other than that my husband is released."

"But your reputation. You are nothing without that."

"Oh, but I am. I am the beloved wife of a man I love. That, sir, is all I need."

He tilted his head to one side. "And you would do this? Tell the world about us?"

Anger flared. "There is no 'us'. But I will tell the world what you did to me and my family. I will tell the world, and you will no longer be entrusted with your position. People will not stand for it, the King will not stand for it."

"The King cares little of such tender scruples."

"He will when the barons combine to make him see. You are under the misapprehension that you and the King are all powerful. You are not, sir. He needs us, he needs my money, and he will only get it if my husband is freed. If you stand in the way of this, then you will be shamed out of office, and I will win anyway."

"And you truly believe I would be ruined by such gossip? For that is what it is. Your word against mine."

"You will be ruined, but I can also give you something you've long wanted."

"You're offering your body to me now?" He laughed. "I've had the best of it. There's nothing more you can give me which I covet."

She shuddered but kept to her purpose. "The de Courcy castle—my family home. I will grant it to you, and its lands, if you free William."

He bit his lip, and his narrow eyes flickered around the room, making sure no one had heard their exchange. Then he glanced at her, his gaze sliding away from her, unable to hold her steady gaze. And she knew she had him then. It was the sweetener that he'd be unable to refuse.

He nodded. "I will do as you say. It will be easier all around."

"Call your clerks. I will wait while you instruct them to free William."

It was strange to sit back and watch her father's cousin—the man who'd robbed her of her youth and innocence, and, she'd thought for many years, her future—do as she bid. But he did. The work was quickly done, and the clerk dispatched to the courts. Only then did he address her once more.

"I will ride immediately to lay claim to your castle."

"You may do as you wish."

He grunted. "You have rescued your husband. What a

good little wife you are. I hope he's happy with his bargain." He leaned forward, and she inhaled his evil breath. "His life, in return for marriage to a used and impoverished woman, who is no doubt as frozen and lifeless in bed as she was with me." He grunted a laugh.

"He loves me."

"You are wrong. You're worthless and used. I loved you once, and no one will love you as I did."

"You call that love?" Her voice was hoarse, and she felt sick. "You have no understanding of the word." She couldn't stay a moment longer. She rose and took a copy of the clerk's missive from his hands. "You can say what you like. You always did. It meant nothing then, and it means nothing now. I pity you for you'll never know happiness, for your lusts will never be sated."

He narrowed his eyes as if he understood her meaning, but then he waved his hand in dismissal. She tarried no longer.

William returned from Norwich with his squire. He was released before dawn while the world was sleeping, to find Warin waiting for him who, alone in the world, appeared to be expecting his release. After a short stop for victuals, they were on the road, galloping back to Wanham.

He asked Warin one question only, and Warin had the grace to answer honestly. It was an answer which William had expected. He'd felt it deep inside. This release wasn't Savari's doing. It required more than diplomacy and knowing the right people. It had been Alice's doing. She'd always refused to reveal to William the identity of the man who'd stolen her innocence. William had had his suspicions, and they'd been confirmed when he'd seen the look in her eyes at court when it had been announced that

William's future lay in the hands of the new Sheriff of Norfolk and Suffolk—Sir Bayard of Wrotham. And it seemed Alice had done something to appease Bayard. It made William sick to his stomach to imagine what that might be. He didn't know, but he was damned sure he'd find out.

ALICE WAS HOLDING the baby as she paced the forecourt in the early hours, wondering if William would ever come, when she heard the sound of horses' hooves. It could be none other than William. Anyone else would wait until it was fully daylight rather than traverse the causeway in the dark.

From the shelter of the gatehouse, she looked across the misty, dim landscape. Hidden under the shroud of darkness, she watched his figure grow, his shape darker than the slowly lightening sky.

The babe hushed in her arms as if also aware that his father was approaching and all would be well from now on.

"Who's there?" he asked, as he pulled his horse up sharply. Before Alice could reply, he tilted his head. "Alice?"

She ran from the shelter toward him. Warin continued into the bailey. "William! It is I, and Charles." She held up the babe, who gave a surprised squawk.

William slipped off his horse and took them both in his arms. He kissed her hard on the lips as if needing to be sure of her presence. He held her face in his hands and looked down at her. She could see the grime and tiredness streaked on his face and the wonderment in his eyes as he drank his fill of her. It warmed her as nothing else could.

"Thank the Lord you are safe," she said, scarcely able to believe he was home again. Safe, with her. For the first time in forever, she began to imagine that they might, just might, be allowed to be happy together.

"The Lord?" he questioned, smoothing her bottom lip with his thumb. "It had little to do with him, did it, Alice?"

Alice was saved from answering by a shriek from inside the castle. Lora poked her head through the courtyard window and brought his sisters running.

William released Alice and greeted everyone. Alice kissed her babe and held him against her shoulder as she watched her husband—*her husband*—she had to repeat the magical words to herself, return to his family. She didn't want this moment to end.

But then he turned to her and gave her a look for her alone, and she knew which way his mind was turning. Any doubts about her role in his release had been firmly pushed to the back of his mind, overtaken by a lust that heated her skin and fluttered and tweaked something deep inside of her. She inhaled a shuddering breath. He held out his hand, and she went to him.

But it wasn't until an hour later, after he'd caught up with everyone and eaten and drank, that he and Alice were able to retire to the bedchamber alone. Once the maid had poured buckets of warm water into the bath, Alice dismissed her. She came to him and took off his jacket and kissed him. Then she ran her fingers under his shirt and pressed her cheek against the rough material, listening to his heart beat under her good ear. She turned and pressed her deaf ear, and smiled.

"What makes you smile, wife?"

"I can hear you through my deaf ear." She frowned. "Not so much a sound, but a feeling in my head."

He stepped out of his clothes, and she tried to hold on to him. He growled. "Release me, Alice, or else the bath will go to waste. I would rid myself of the grime of the gaol before I come to you."

She laughed and let him go. He stepped into the steaming

tub and slipped under the water, allowing the water to cover him entirely. When he surfaced, she rubbed soap over his shoulders and chest, kissing the clean skin.

Once he was clean, she rinsed him off with a bucket of cool water. He stepped out, dripping. She offered him a drying cloth, and he shook his head. "There's only one thing I want now, wife. And that's to make you as wet as I am."

She stepped back but not quickly enough, and he wrapped his large wet arms around her, and she squealed. But not for long because soon his mouth claimed hers, kissing her with an intensity which robbed her mind of thought. And when his hands explored her body, he found her as wet as he wanted to make her.

MUCH LATER, they lay tangled on the bed, sated from sex, listening to the everyday sounds of the castle. In silence, they watched the shifting patterns of sunlight move across the oak ceiling and the stone walls. She felt bathed in light, from outside and within. She sighed and shifted a little, fully aware that, at some point, she needed to tell him something he had no wish to hear.

She kissed his chest, and he placed his chin on the top of her head. She listened to his breathing, steady and sure and strong. It was now or never.

"William," she said quietly.

He kissed her head. "Alice," he said.

She couldn't speak, and the silence lengthened.

He shifted and tried to look at her face. "Why are we stating each other's names?" She could hear the smile in his voice.

She lifted her head. "Because I have something to tell you."

She hated the way his smile dropped from his lips. He didn't say anything, simply waited for her to continue.

"I went to see the Sheriff."

He sucked in a breath and nodded. "Yes, I know. Warin told me."

She jolted upright. "Warin told you?"

"Of course, he had no choice. But what I don't know is what you did to convince him to release me. And I'm not sure I want to know."

She suddenly realized what he suspected.

She shook her head. "I made a deal with him, but not, I suspect, the kind you imagine."

He blinked and sighed. "If it were not that kind of deal, then what?"

"I gave him what he coveted—my castle. He will be there by now. He was anxious to lay claim to it."

"Your castle," he said quietly. "It is a lot. But we have our own home here, so we do not need another. And was that enough for him?"

She shook her head.

"Did you have some kind of hold over him?"

"Aye," she whispered. "I held secrets."

"And so you promised to keep them if, in return, he set me free."

She bit her cheek and blinked. "Yes."

The fire crackled, and minutes passed before he pulled his arms away from her and sat up in bed, staring straight ahead. "And these secrets..." He stopped talking as if it pained him. He stood up and pulled on his shirt before turning to her. "It was him, wasn't it? It was he who hurt you so many years ago. The man whose identity you refused to tell me. It was him."

It wasn't a question. William knew.

Alice bit her lip and nodded anxiously.

William turned from her, and Alice couldn't read his thoughts. But she saw him flex his hands. It wasn't a good sign.

"But, William. The matter has been dealt with. You mustn't do anything. You've only just..."

He shot her a look over his shoulder, softening it immediately when his eyes met hers. "Only just been released from prison. Because my wife gave her abuser a gift—the gift of secrecy." He swallowed hard. "So no one will ever know what he did to you. So he can retain everyone's good opinion, his wealth, his status, and carry on as if he didn't hurt the woman I love."

She nodded, and a tear trickled down her cheek as she realized exactly how hurt he was by her actions.

He didn't attempt to wipe away her tears as he'd always done. "You know it cannot be left like this."

"Please," she sobbed. "William, I cannot bear to lose you again."

"You will only lose me if you do not allow me to protect me and mine. I cannot leave it like this."

And with that, he left the room, leaving Alice to cry tears which could no longer move him.

CHAPTER 17

It took all of William's will power to stop himself from getting back on his horse, riding over to Bayard and dealing with him immediately. But he knew he couldn't rush in. He had to think. So, instead, he took himself out onto the land he loved and breathed deeply of the late spring air, forcing himself to pay attention to the new growth on the trees, and in the land. The fresh green sprouts which had emerged from the cold dark soil of early spring were flourishing, having waited their time until the sun had warmth. Timing was everything. And he had to have patience, at least until he'd put his thoughts in order.

He'd soon left the shadow of the castle behind him. He knew Alice would be upset, but there was no point in returning. She wouldn't be able to make him change his mind. He needed to act, and he needed her not to stop him. So he continued toward the river. There were people there, he knew, who would be only too pleased to help him.

THE MEN who lived and worked on the rivers and marshes

were expecting him. He'd made sure of that. He'd also made sure they were fully aware of what had happened, and to whom. He'd known they'd be interested and that they'd help him. They had no love for the man who'd murdered their elder—the island hermit who'd died helping William's family and their own people escape the tyranny of the de Montmorency clan—the same man who'd robbed Alice of her innocence and nearly, her future.

No, William had had no qualms about revealing everything that had happened to Alice and himself concerning Bayard of Wrotham. Now wasn't the time for secrets; it was the time for action.

Their meeting didn't last long. It was as he'd imagined. Both he and the river men hated the sheriff with a vengeance and the plan he'd conjured in the course of a few hours had the advantage of being both simple—using the river men's strengths, capitalizing on their ability to move easily and unnoticed over the marsh Norfolk lands—and effective.

He waited with Warin and the river men, finessing the details of their plan until the day had begun to wane. As the sun slipped behind the top of the trees, which ringed the group of huts by the river, William rose, stretched, and inhaled the chill watery air of those low lands. It was cold. But he relished this kind of cold—cold that was outside, cold that was of the earth and the water, not a gaol of weeping walls.

As he left the river men's encampment, he knew they were also on the move. He barely heard them—only a whisper as they pushed their boats onto the rising river, only a flapping of wings of the marsh birds, disturbed from behind the reeds as they flew off into the darkening sky. That was all to indicate the river men, too, were on their way, spreading out like a spider's web behind William, making sure that what he started, they would end.

It wasn't far to de Courcy Castle. With every cantered step, one thought only filled his mind—he would make sure that the man who'd hurt his woman never had the chance to do so again.

William and Warin reined in their mounts outside the gatehouse, which was locked. He'd been told it would be locked—it made the new owner feel secure—but he also knew that the men and women within were expecting them. They knew what to do. He didn't turn around to see if the men were in position. A high-pitched bird call confirmed it.

They dismounted, and when they reached the gatehouse, it swung open quietly, admitting them both. The person who had opened it said nothing and immediately retreated into the shadows. William caught sight of two men guarding the gatehouse and heard muffled cries coming from beneath the guardhouse, where the gaol pit was. They'd be released when this was over. He'd given orders for no one else to be harmed.

He gave his horse to his squire and told him to stay and be ready. William took one last look around and walked across the bailey yard to the stairs, which led up to the Great Hall. He had no intention of entering from the rear door, as he'd been counseled by the river men. He'd be doing this the right way, entering through the main door, and meeting his enemy head-on.

He ran up the stairs, opened the door, and stepped inside. It had always been a dark Hall, even when Alice and her family had lived there, but now the air seemed denser somehow, except the fire wasn't smoking. It took him two scans of the Hall, clothed in the strange gloom, to see the man he sought.

He sat alone. William hadn't expected that.

"About time!" Bayard called out. "You should have come immediately! Where the hell is everyone, anyway?"

William walked up to him, and slowly Bayard turned to him. It was all William could do not to take the man by the scruff of the neck and throw him to the ground. But that wasn't the way. He knew that now. Alice had shown him that. The man jumped up when he saw who it was who approached him. Fear registered in his face as he looked around, but there was no one there to help him, as William had arranged.

"Sir William! I did not expect company this night!" William could hear an edge of panic to his voice.

"And I, also, had not expected to spend my first night in Norfolk away from Wanham."

Bayard called out for a servant, but no one came. "I'd offer you a drink, but it looks like the servants are busy."

"Or, mayhap, they're not here."

Bayard stumbled away, spilling the remains of his drink on the rushes. He took another step toward the chest where his cloak had been tossed. William knew that he was hoping to reach his sword.

"So what brings you here, Sir William, when you could be at home with your fair wife."

A surge of anger burst through William at the mention of Alice. "Do not speak of her," he roared.

Bayard shook his head and licked his lips. "Of course. It seems you are angered that I now own the castle."

"Believe me, it is not that which angers me."

"Then I suggest you calm yourself, and tell me the reason you're here."

"The reason? You!"

"Me?" He swallowed again as if his mouth had suddenly drained of moisture. "What could you possibly want with me?" His voice was now hoarse with fear. He grappled behind him for a sword or dagger, which William knew was no longer there.

"Want? I'd like to do many things as it happens."

"You wouldn't dare! My men are close by, as are the servants."

"I think you'll find there are none here."

"Of course they are here. I haven't given them—" He stopped abruptly and called out, louder than before, panic giving his voice strength. The call turned into a shout, which turned into a screech as Bayard realized the truth of William's words. The sound made the hairs on the back of William's neck rise.

He turned to William. "What have you done to them?"

"I?" William shrugged. "I have done nothing. I believe they decided they'd rather be outside on this fine evening, rather than here, with you."

"They are *my* servants!" he thundered. "I did not give them leave!"

"No, but *I* did." William gestured for Bayard to take a seat. "Sit, I would speak to you."

Bayard turned to the chest and, no longer caring for subterfuge, swept the cloak from the top to discover his weapons were no longer there. He turned back to William, gripping the chest and cowering, his eyes dark with anger and fear. "Where are my people!" Spittle formed at the corners of his mouth as he ranted.

"They were never your people. They owe allegiance to Lady Alice's family, and, as her husband, to me. They are of the land, as am I. You are an interloper here. You are not welcome."

"This place has been given to me. Lady Alice gave it to me."

"To pay you off."

"And I freed you, did I not? I kept my side of the bargain."

"Ah, but I have a new bargain for us to make."

"And why should I? I have everything I need here."

William scoffed. "You are not welcome here."

"If the de Courcy servants don't wish to stay, I can soon replace them."

"No, you misunderstand me. *I* do not welcome you."

"You do not own this castle."

"*That* is not in dispute. I don't wish to own it. I have enough. What I will not have is the man who made Alice's life hell, who raped her, beat her and abused her most vilely, live so close to us— to *her*."

Bayard's creased face whitened under the trim gray beard. "Whatever I did—and you cannot prove anything—was done because she wanted it!"

This time William couldn't stop himself. All thought and control flew from his mind as rage consumed him, and he launched his fist into the man's neat beard, sending him flying to the floor. A dog jumped up, yelping in surprise from before the fire, and a flagon of wine tipped over, dripping onto Bayard's head.

"Don't," said William, breathing deeply, willing the control he'd been holding onto all afternoon, control he'd been counseled to keep, to surface once more. It took half a dozen breaths and some swearing before he had managed to calm himself. "Don't you ever say such a thing again."

"Why not, if it's…"

Before Bayard could finish what he was going to say, he must have seen the fury in William's eyes. So, instead, Bayard righted himself and rubbed his chin. William stepped away and turned from the sight of the man whom he wanted to kill. But whose death by his hands would ruin not only his future but the future of the woman he loved.

Suddenly William was knocked over as Bayard lunged at him, obviously not as stunned by William's blow as he'd wanted to appear. His hands were around William's neck in a desperate grip, and William couldn't breathe.

But Bayard was no match for William, and William easily prized his fingers away before throwing him across the Hall, slamming him against the unforgiving stone wall.

Bayard lay panting and dazed while William rubbed his neck and swallowed with difficulty and looked at Bayard. There was no way he'd be taking his eyes off him again.

"You will not win a one-on-one fight against me," said William in a measured tone, willing himself to retain control. "So do not try."

The man lay panting on the ground. He looked up from all fours like the animal he was, and scowled.

"What would you have me do?"

"Leave England. Leave these shores where you are not wanted and disappear into far lands."

"What if I do not wish it?" He staggered to his feet and tried to show bravado, but the effect was pathetic. "I have friends, you know."

"Fairweather friends. They'll not stand by you now." William approached him. Bayard stepped back, fear now showing clearly in his eyes. "Let me put it this way. If you stay here another hour, I'll kill you myself."

"You will hang."

"I do not care. It'll be worth the price."

The man shook his head, narrowing his bloodshot eyes, blood trickling from his nose. "You love her that much?"

"I love her more than life itself."

The man grunted. "She said as much, and I told her that she was wrong. I told her she was worthless, and no one would love her as I had."

William heard the bellow and hardly registered it was from himself. Darkness swallowed his vision, and it was only when his squire pulled him off the now senseless man that he realized he'd lost control yet again.

"Take him away before I kill him!"

Two river men appeared from the shadows, looking like river wraiths, skinny, with long hair and the characteristic short coat and flat-topped hats of their people. They hoisted Bayard to his feet and, half-supporting him, half-dragging him, pulled him toward the door.

"Stop!" William called.

The men stopped, and Bayard turned to him. He looked maniacal in the sputtering torchlight. Blood trickled down his cheek. "You want to kill me after all?" He spat onto the hard ground.

"No, I'd have done so if I were going to. The only reason I haven't is that Alice wouldn't want me to."

"Alice," the man said derisively.

William ignored the jibe. "You will leave this country and never set foot in it again. Do you understand?"

For one long moment, they eyed each other, and William felt the depths of the man's evil.

"Do you understand?" William repeated.

"Aye, I understand." He looked around the castle and up at the dark skies. "I've always hated the damned place anyway. I think I'll find me a widow with children somewhere where I can while away my time. Find some amusement."

William recoiled. "Take him away."

As he watched him leave, his squire joined him. "Do you think he'll have a future as he imagines? It pains me to see such an evil man prosper."

William turned to his squire, still so young in thought and deed, despite his experience. "Warin. Bayard killed the hermit, a river man like the men who now take him away. They do not hold to laws, to our forms of justice. They do things their own way."

Warin's eyes widened in the dark.

"I did not kill him," continued William. "But he *will* be

killed and the only trace is his name booked on an outward voyage to Lisbon."

Wearily, William walked out of the Hall and into the yard, where he washed the blood from his hands at the pump. He gave one last look around the castle which had been the setting of so much suffering for his beloved, and knew he'd never set foot in the place ever again.

As he mounted his horse, he was aware of people emerging from all parts of the castle. When he turned to face them, the men inclined their heads and slowly doffed their caps, while the women curtseyed, low and deep. They were honoring him, he realized. But, more than that, they were honoring his lady.

He nodded to them, thankful they would be free from the tyrant. Who would take ownership now, he had no idea. But if it were up to these people, it would be Alice. Perhaps it would return to Alice, perhaps not. He had no mind to care, but he knew who would. For Alice's sake, and for the sake of the people and servants and guards who'd helped him this day, he'd ask Savari to tie up the legal ends. Savari would use his legal and political expertise to make sure the castle was returned to the rightful owner.

And that was the last thought he gave it as he and Warin cantered across the dark fields, back to Wanham, back to his Alice, safe at last.

CHAPTER 18

When Alice awoke, she found William asleep in bed beside her. She'd waited as long as she could the previous evening for him to return, but couldn't bear the tension, the things that were unsaid between the sisters, the darting, anxious looks at her. And she'd felt increasingly unwell, so she'd retired to bed. There she'd lain awake for hours, ears straining for the slightest sound which would indicate William was returning, alive and well. But the exhaustion which pulled at her limbs finally won, and she'd fallen into a heavy sleep before he'd returned.

The feeling of tiredness and nausea remained, despite his safe return. And even now, as she looked down at William, the queasiness remained. She poured a cup of weak ale and sat sipping it, her eyes feasting on William, who had pulled off only his boots before lying on the bed fully clothed.

Relief filled her. Despite her questions, he'd refused to tell her where he'd been going the previous day. He'd never done that before, never kept anything from her, which had made her even more afraid. Because it had meant two things—wherever he'd been going it had been important, and it involved her. And there could only be one reason why he hadn't told her what he was about—she would have tried to stop him.

She rose and stood over him. He lay on his back, in the same position as he'd fallen upon the bed. The one exception was the hand which even now reached out for her. She'd awoken with it around her waist. She watched the play of the low sunlight, streaming in through the unshuttered window, upon his face, revealing the softness of the man which he kept hidden when he was awake. He was a stern, strong man with a loving heart and soul. She loved this man. He was as dependable as the land around them and as constant. He loved her, too; she knew that now. She'd known it the moment he'd agreed to let her go to follow her misplaced desires to live at the Priory and become a nun.

She closed her eyes in a slight panic at the way her life would have gone if that had happened. She'd have never known the magic of his touch against hers, the beauty their two bodies created. She touched her stomach. The life it had created.

Then she saw blood on William's clothes. Gently, so as not to awaken him, she pulled his clothes away and breathed easily once more when she found no wound. But, she thought, if it wasn't William's blood, whose was it?

What had he done?

It was the sunlight that awoke William. He blinked, wondering where he was. Then he reached out for Alice only to find her gone. Panic thumped through his veins, and he leaped up, alert and ready. He looked around to see Alice, seated, watching him.

He tugged in a deep breath. "Why did you not wake me? I should have been out hours since."

"You were sleeping so well, I supposed you needed it."

He pushed his hands through his unruly hair. "By the rood, I never sleep like that. Even if I'm up all night."

"No. I suspect last night you slept well because you were satisfied. Your spirit was calm." She rose. "Well, William, your spirit shouldn't have been calm. You went behind my back."

There was something warm and lovely about his quiet Alice being a possessive wife. He smiled. He suddenly realized that it was a mistake.

"Why do you smile? Do you think it amusing to leave your sisters and me at home, worried half to death as to what you might be doing? Worried," she said, with a slight choke in her voice, "that you might not return. Hey? Do you find that amusing?"

That she could stand there and be free to hector him, he *did* find not exactly amusing, but heartwarming and reassuring, but he realized now wasn't the time to tell her. He managed to suppress the smile which tweaked at his lips. "No, of course not, my love." He decided avoidance was his best tactic. He glanced out the window. "Anyhow, why did you not awaken me?" he asked, sitting on the bed and pulling on his boots. "I should have been out and about long since."

"Not so fast, William de Vere."

He rose and came over to her, unable to prevent the smile now from curving his lips as he took in her flushed face and the determined jut of her jaw.

He pushed back the hair from her face and laced his fingers behind her head, holding her steady so he could admire those beautiful lips. "Not so fast?" He pressed his lips against hers, which softened reassuringly to his touch before he pulled away. "Hmm, I can go as slow as you like, my love. Come to think of it, business can wait."

She gripped his hands and threw them away. He frowned. She'd never acted like this before.

"Not before you tell me where you've been."

He shrugged. "To sort out a problem."

"A problem." He didn't like the way she repeated his words. Nor did he like the way she folded her arms and tapped her foot. "A problem," she again repeated. His heart dropped.

"Aye, as I say. It's sorted, so it doesn't bear repeating."

She put her hands on her hips in an entirely new manner. Again, he only just managed to prevent a smile. His vulnerable beauty of a wife had come far. He wondered what he could continue to do to receive the same nagging, day in day out, for the rest of his life. It would be a reminder to him of how far she'd come, returned to the girl he'd fallen in love with so many years before.

"Mayhap in your mind it doesn't bear repeating, but I'd ask that you do."

"Would you, now?" He couldn't help teasing.

"Aye, I would." He could tell by the firm set of her lips that she wasn't going to let it go.

"Well, then. I went to your castle."

"It is not my castle anymore. And well you know."

"I know nothing of the sort."

Her eyes narrowed in what he imagined was suspicion and anger, but which he couldn't help thinking made her look even sexier than she usually did. "And what, pray, do you mean by that?"

"Simply that the castle will be yours once more."

"What have you done, William?" She barely breathed the words.

"I've dealt with the outstanding matter of your castle."

"There was nothing outstanding about it. I had settled the matter."

Now it was his turn to see red. "Settled? You went behind my back and decided that bribing that, that *monster* would be the only way to buy my freedom." He pointed his finger at her. "I don't need my freedom to be bought."

She grabbed hold of his finger, sparks lighting her blue eyes. "Don't you ever waggle your finger at me, William de Vere." She gripped it hard, and the anger faded as quickly as it had risen. Her soft fingers around his calloused ones made him forget everything except the lovely woman before him. He tried to stop the tweak of amusement from twitching the corners of his mouth. But must have failed because he saw a corresponding softening in her face. "You could have been killed," she added softly.

"But I wasn't."

She licked her lips, suddenly hesitant. "Did you…" She trailed off, as she gave a slight grimace, unable to give voice to her fears.

"Did I kill him?" He shook his head. "No, my love, I didn't. I have no desire to be thrown into gaol again, to lose you, to lose my life over someone as worthless as that man."

She frowned. "So he's still alive?" Fear flickered across her face, and he kissed first one cheek and then another, hating to see the old Alice return so easily. He knew then that no matter how steady, secure, and loving her life would be in the future, the scars would always remain. But mayhap, with each year they would heal further, would become less livid, more easily forgotten. He vowed he'd do anything to make that happen.

He shook his head. "No, he's not alive. I told him he could leave and leave he did. Alone. Straight into the hands of the river men. He found they were not as merciful as me."

She closed her eyes and took a steadying breath. "So he's gone."

"Aye, he's gone. The men never forgave him for killing the old hermit."

"I pray they made it swift."

"I do not. My only prayer is that the body won't be found. And my prayers will be answered, for the river is a cruel mistress, especially when a body is weighted with stones."

"Oh, William. You risked so much! You could have been killed, and I couldn't have born that."

"I know how to look after myself. You shouldn't have worried. Besides, I couldn't let him stay. He would have always been a threat to you, a reminder of what"—he was at a loss for words on how to describe the horrors the man had perpetrated—"of went before."

"But we need you, William. I could have lived with that man nearby so long as you were with us."

"You may have done, but I could not." He frowned as her words ran through his mind over and over. There was something he wasn't understanding. On the second run through his mind faltered over the "we". She'd said *we* rather than *me*. "You mean you and my sisters."

He'd said it as a statement, for who else could she have meant?

She licked her lips. "No, I do not." She shrugged. "Although of course, they love you. But they will leave and go live their own lives, in time."

He frowned as she turned away. She never turned away from him, always looked him in the eye. The tables had been turned. From her prevarication, he now knew she was hiding something from him. And, like his secret, he knew hers would be important.

"Alice, look at me," he called softly. She turned to him, and what he saw in her eyes puzzled him further. There was disbelief, laughter, and a kind of pure joy that he didn't understand.

"Then who did you mean? You said 'we'."

"Me and our child."

He breathed out. "Of course. Charles. Where is he?"

"He slept beside Lora last night. We didn't know when you'd return, and didn't want to disturb him."

William grunted his assent. When Charles awoke in the night, the whole castle knew about it. He shook his head. "I cannot believe it has all come to pass. You, our child, and the land. It is everything I've always wanted."

Alice smiled and ran her finger across his lips before kissing him. "Everything?" she asked in what he could only name as a seductive and sexy voice. It wasn't one she'd used before. It seemed the removal of Bayard had lifted the last layer Alice had put between herself and the world. "I think there may be something else you want."

He raised an eyebrow. "Aye, well, that's a given." He reached out and grabbed her by the waist and pulled her onto his lap where she could discover exactly how much he wanted her.

She laughed, and he pulled her closer and kissed her. When she pulled away, she placed a hand on his shoulder, stopping him from following up the kiss with more intimate caresses.

"Nay, not yet, William. I would show you something."

He narrowed his eyes, all attention. "Go ahead. I'll gladly look at anything you care to show me."

To his surprise, she jumped up and unclasped the light robe she wore and let it fall to the floor with an abandon she'd only just acquired. She wore only her shift when she took his hand and pulled him to standing, and began taking off his clothes. It seemed only courteous for William to help her.

He soon stood naked, and reached out to rid her of the only piece of clothing she wore now, a shift beneath which he could see the outline of her body. But she shook her head and pushed him back onto the bed.

She sat on his lap and kissed him, and he forgot about

everything except the way her bottom caressed him and the peaks of her breasts, which pushed through the soft cloth of her chemise. He pulled down her chemise and took one of the dark buds in his mouth and suckled her, harder than he'd ever done before. But then, before, she'd always looked more vulnerable, and he'd not wanted to hurt or frighten her. But now it looked as if she had control and was enjoying it.

She gasped and inhaled deeply, her breasts rising, allowing him to fill his mouth with her, to allow his tongue to lave and explore that which she pushed into him. She dropped her head back, and he exposed her other breast, playing with it with his fingers before moving his mouth to that one.

She seemed far more sensitive than usual, and suddenly she twisted around and placed one leg either side of his body, allowing him easier reach to her breasts and her naked sex—the chemise having ridden up to the top of her legs—pressed against his cock.

As his mouth latched onto her nipples, first one than the other, she writhed against him, pleasuring herself as she pushed against his hardness. She moved more and more quickly, her breathing come in short, hard pants before she cried out, and he felt the moisture leak from her and onto him. It was more than he could stand.

With one swift movement, she was on her back, and he'd plunged deep inside of her, still feeling the waves of pleasure caressing him, pulling him, wanting him. And he wanted to give her everything he had. And he did.

But after they both came, it seemed once wasn't to be enough for his lady. Alice was on fire with desire, and while they were still connected, he followed her lead and rolled onto his back. She sat astride him, moving on him, closing her eyes as the movements pleasured her, her hands reaching and caressing his muscles and sinews. She leaned down and kissed his chest, licking his nipples as he'd done hers. His cock was soon hard inside her again. But he knew it wouldn't be over so quickly this time. Both of them had been pleasured, now they could take their time.

And, it seemed, Alice was in charge. She ground down upon him, lifted up, following some age-old sense, watching his pleasure and experimenting, repeating when she saw his reaction. Then she nodded, and a slow smile spread over her face. With both hands, she lifted her chemise from her body and placed his hands upon her stomach.

"This is the 'we', William. Me and our baby."

He heard the words but couldn't believe them straight away. She had to repeat them before he fully understood.

"For years, I never imagined such a thing would come to pass."

He smiled. "That's what happens when you love someone."

"Love..." She repeated dreamily. He kissed her, preventing further talk, as his lips and tongue coaxed her to demand another, very physical, kind of loving. And he gave it to her, more gently than she wanted, but he made sure she was satisfied, for she would be the mother of his children. And he'd make sure to honor her and protect them all.

EPILOGUE

Richard William de Vere, first natural-born son of Sir William and Lady Alice of Wanham, was born when the leaves had turned yellow and had fallen to the earth which his father so loved. The castle storerooms were full to the brim with sweet apples, and pears plucked from Wanham trees, grain from the fields, and salted fish and meat, ready for the winter ahead.

William looked down at his bonny boy, and vowed, not for the first time, to make sure he lived a full, happy, and honorable life. Tears pricked his eyes.

"William!" exclaimed Alice, sweeping into the room with Charles on her hip. "I do believe your children are the only people who can bring you to tears!"

William cleared his throat. "Nonsense. I was only ensuring he was well. He lies there without sound. I thought he might be sickening for something."

"As you see," replied Alice, "he is hale and happy."

"And also very quiet."

"Like his father. And like you, he'll follow you onto the land and care for it and his people." She kissed Charles and put him on the rug. He promptly crawled off with a loping movement, which made them both laugh.

"And what will young Charles do with his life, I wonder?" said William. "He's certainly not as quiet as Richard."

"Charles will have the de Courcy castle, as we've arranged."

They both fell silent. Neither spoke of the past if they could help it, only the future.

"Aye, he'll have that, if he wishes it. But there's something about him which makes me think he might not stay. He has the spirit of an adventurer. Like Rufus."

"It is because of Rufus I came looking for you and Katherine," said Alice. William knew she was changing the subject. She did not like to think of a time when her boys would leave her. He took her hand and pulled her onto his lap and kissed her. He reasoned it would help push the unpleasant thought of her boys leaving her further from her mind.

Eventually, with a frustrated sigh that he could not ravish her there and then, he pulled away. "So, what is it about Rufus?"

It took Alice a few moments to re-focus, which she did with a deeply inhaled breath. She nodded as her mind retraced her thoughts.

"Ah, we've received a letter, and he has a question of trade for you and Katherine. I thought she might be here."

"I haven't seen her since yesterday. She left for Yarmouth early. It seems business is taking her more frequently to Yarmouth these days."

Alice frowned. "Come to think of it, I didn't see her when I returned late from Norwich last night. I took the boys straight to bed." Her frown deepened. "You do not think she didn't return home?"

"She must have done. If not, she'll return by day's end. She never stays away for more than one night."

Alice grunted, and William could tell she was worried. She rose and went to the unshuttered window which gave a view across the flat lands to the city of Yarmouth. He joined her and put a comforting arm around her.

"All will be well, you'll see. No doubt more issues with this sea Captain who's been causing her trouble."

"No doubt," she repeated, but from the tone of her voice, he knew she wasn't convinced.

Both their gazes turned in the direction of Yarmouth, which was becoming hazy as a sea fret rolled in.

"I hope she makes it back before the fret turns thicker, and the road becomes more treacherous," said Alice.

"So do I," replied William, closing the shutters upon the increasingly chill air. "So do I," he repeated, not wanting to assign meaning to the flicker of fear in his belly.

Dear Reader,

I hope you enjoyed William and Alice's story. Katherine and her mysterious captain's story is next. You can sign up to my newsletter to receive news of its publication.

Reviews are always welcome—they help me, and they help prospective readers to decide if they'd enjoy the book.

For news on forthcoming books or to sign up to my newsletter, please check out my website—http://www.saskiaknight.com.

Happy reading!

Saskia

ALSO BY SASKIA KNIGHT

—Norfolk Knights—

Novellas

Claiming his Lady (Book 1)

Seducing his Lady (Book 2)

Awakening his Lady (Book 3)

Full-Length Books

Defending his Lady (Book 4)

Honoring his Lady (Book 5)

Printed in Great Britain
by Amazon

51835157R00130